T0121219

Hannibal Lecter, My Father

Hannibal Lecter, My Father

KATHY ACKER

Edited by Sylvère Lotringer

Semiotext(e) Native Agents Series

"Politics." (fragment) Unpublished, 1968.

"New York City in 1979." Top Stories No.9, 1981.

"Lust." First published in The Seven Deadly Sins, Serpents Tail, 1981.

"The Birth of the Poet," 1981. First published in Performance Arts Journal, 1986.

"Translations of the Diaries of Laure the Schoolgirl." First published in Diana's, 1983.

"Algeria." First published in Aloes Books London, 1984.

Special thanks to Peter Gente, Jeanine Herman, Frank Mecklenburg,
Heidi Paris, Jordan Zinovich.

Design & Text Production: Kim Spurlock @ Art&Language

Cover design: Hedi El Kholti

Semiotext(e)

2007 Wilshire Blvd., Suite 427

Los Angeles, Ca 90057

www.semiotexte.com

ISBN 978-0-936756-68-4

We gratefully acknowledge
financial assistance in the
publication of this book from the
New York State Council on the Arts.

CONTENTS

Hannibal Lecter, My Father

DEVOURED BY MYTHS
AN INTERVIEW WITH SYLVÈRE LOTRINGER

"Modern myths are even less understood than ancient myths, although we're devoured by myths."—Balzac

MIXED UP MEMORIES

LOTRINGER: Before I met you I had heard of that writer called the Black Tarantula. I was very intrigued. Actually you were pretty different from what I had imagined. Why did you take that name in the first place?

ACKER: I was living in Frisco with Peter—Peter Gordon—in the Haight-Ashbury section right after the hippy period. The section was a very whoopy town for about two years and then it became gay and started to spruce up. There was a wonderful theater group that used to be the Coquettes and changed to the Angels of Light. Some of the Angels of Light lived up the street from us and I became friendly with them. According to the guide every bar at the time was gay, but it wasn't quite true. It was this ambiance in which everyone was androgynous. You weren't gay, you weren't straight, it was very loose. And everybody changed their name, everybody dressed up all the time, everybody wore make-up.

LOTRINGER: Even Peter Gordon?

ACKER: Peter enjoyed watching. Peter's eyes got very big at all this. I would go up the street for these orgies, Peter never came. I remember I had a girlfriend for a time, Vanessa, who used to sing with Prissy Condition. Vanessa was this beautiful, beautiful black girl and she would come in and whop Peter around. She would say, I'm gonna fuck your girlfriend now and Peter would just gig-

1

gle. He didn't know what else to do. Ah, Vanessa was something. I was writing but I didn't want to make a thing about it. It was as if I had two lives. I hung around them and also was a writer. So I made up a name for myself and that name was Rip-Off Red. And I wrote a novel at that point *Rip-Off Red—Girl Detective*, which is the first novel I've ever written. Very luckily it has never been published. (Laughs). It was a pornographic mystery story and it was supposed to earn me a lot of money in my very deluded brain.

LOTRINGER: How old were you then?

ACKER: When I wrote TARANTULA I was 23, so I was around 22. Where did I write THE BLACK TARANTULA? Oh memory, it gets everything mixed up. I definitely was with Peter when I wrote *Rip-Off Red*. And we were in Frisco. Before that I was doing TARANTULA down in San Diego. I was the Black Tarantula before I was Rip-Off Red. So there goes that apocryphal story.

LOTRINGER: Why the Black Tarantula?

ACKER: I don't remember, I honestly don't. I liked tarantulas in those days and I probably like them now. Mexican kids keep them as pets. And they're really sensual, really soft and furry. Everyone thinks they're horrible, but they're not terribly dangerous. The worst they do is sting like a bee.

LOTRINGER: That was quite a punk name.

ACKER: Yeah, but this was way before punk. I guess I wasn't a very good hippy. We just liked the Velvet Underground—we didn't have anyone really to like in those days. Well, I eat like a hippy, but I never really was into free love. I am just not that loose. And in those days the men really had all the power, all they did is to get these women pregnant. It wasn't really much fun, you end up with five babies and no boyfriend.

LOTRINGER: Was that the first time you went to California?

ACKER: Yeah. I went to school in San Diego. I studied Greek and Latin. Then we lived in San Francisco for two years where Peter was studying with Bob Ashley. Peter was really a nice guy.

I met him when I first escaped New York in 1973-74 and we lived together until about 1980. Six years, almost seven. A long time. When you met me I was living with Peter and he broke the marriage. So that was... Wait, I can remember exactly because that's when my mother suicided. Three months after the marriage split up. I was 30, so it was twelve years ago.

LOTRINGER: We met in 1977.

ACKER: So I was with Peter from 1970 to 1977? I must have been in California earlier than I thought and I moved out there to live with Peter in 1970. So that gets the dates right.

LOTRINGER: Did you connect to the art world there?

ACKER: David Antin had been my mentor and had introduced me to the early conceptual artists, Dan Graham and Joseph Kosuth. David was very much of a conceptualist.

LOTRINGER: What does it mean, conceptualist, in terms of writing?

ACKER: Most poets in those days didn't think why did they write the way they wrote. There was still, and still is, the lingering idea of good poetry as the perfect word in the perfect line. And what David really taught me is, the hell with all that. Just think what do you want to do and do it. Form is determined not by arbitrary rules, but by intention. And intentionality is all. That's what I meant by this emphasis on conceptualism, on intentionality. So I had really been trained in the idea that you just don't sit down and write, you have to know why you write and why you use certain methodologies.

LOTRINGER: Any other training as a writer?

ACKER: I grew up in New York City and when I was a teenager I was introduced to a lot of the underground filmmakers, Stan Brakhage, Stan Rice, Gregory Markopolos. Most important I met Jack Smith who told me that his dream was to have a huge dome in Africa and anybody would walk and tell their dreams, which I thought was absolutely fabulous. But just as important I was introduced to Robert Kelly and Jackson MacLow and to the work

3

of Charles Olson. So you might say I had an early training in Black Mountain School rhetoric which came mainly out of *The Wasteland* and Pound's work, *The Cantos*. Olson's main thesis was that one sentence comes after another sentence so you might have the movement of meaning, but also a movement where language leads to language. Olson also had his way of seeing the world and putting it down in a certain kind of rhythm, usually a very jagged rhythm, like writing from scat. It all had to do with music.

LOTRINGER: You were writing poetry then?

ACKER: No, I never wrote poetry, I always wanted to write prose. So I was looking for models of fiction that were poetic and fiction writers don't work that way. They outline things before they write. They don't write by process. The only model I found in my world was William Burroughs. I like Kerouac but he worked too much from intuition for me and I wasn't interested in that kind of autobiographical work. Whereas Burroughs really was doing the major work because he was dealing with how politics and language come together, the kind of language, what the image is, all that early Burroughs work. Burroughs was the only prose writer I could find who was a conceptualist. Oh he's very much of a conceptualist. So I used *The Third Mind* as experiments to teach myself how to write, and I think this is part of the trouble I had with the St. Mark's people because this was not the usual thing to do.

LOTRINGER: You had come back to New York by then.

ACKER: Yeah, and I hung out in the poetry scene. That was the St. Mark's Poetry Project. I was working in a sex-show in 42nd Street and I had two lives, the poetry and the sex-show. I was in it only six months but it pretty radically changed my view of the world.

LOTRINGER: In what way?

ACKER: One, it changed my politics. When I was in the university at San Diego I was SDS, but the student left was very elitist. The 42nd Street experience made me learn about street politics. You see people from the bottom up, and sexual behavior, especially sex minus relationship—which is what happens in 42nd Street—is definitely bottom. Then you see it in a different way, especially power relationships in society. Genet has the same kind of perspective. And I think that never left me.

LOTRINGER: What about your other life in the poetry scene?

ACKER: I really wasn't comfortable there. I felt very rejected. The people I was close to were the generation above me—the people who are my age are Larry Fagin, Michael Brownstein. At that point the culture was hippy and all these hippies in the St. Mark's Poetry Project at the time were very much into fucking around with each other and writing about it. The poetry was very autobiographical, very third generation Surrealist, some of it had come down from the New York School. And working in a sex-show really didn't make you feel very nice about sex. It was all about money and that's how I thought about it. It's not that I fucked for work because it was just fake—I performed with this guy Mark Stevens, I think he became a famous porn star, and he was totally gay; if he tried to kiss me, he'd start giggling—but still it was enough. I didn't need it back in the home-base. So I was very separated culturally from these people. And they thought I was weird, I was some kind of a pervert. Everyone was in blue jeans and I had shaved my head—that was my radical stance against working in a sex-show. (Laughs). It wasn't very radical, but what can you do when you need money? I hated men at that point, even though I was living with a guy from the sex-show. He was a real creep anyway.

LOTRINGER: Were you writing at the time?

ACKER: Oh yeah, I was writing. I was writing regularly. I was writing a book called POLITICS, which was little prose poems. In the middle of POLITICS there's a huge diary section—this is what I used to read at St. Mark's—and in the diary section I wasn't dealing with a fake I, with fake autobiography yet, I was cutting in tapes, cutting out tapes, using a lot of dream material, using other people's dreams, doing a lot of Burroughs experiments. It was all about the sex shows, with cut-in dreams, cut-in politics, cut-in everything. A few big publishers came around but I think they just loved the sensationalism of it. I thought if this gets published in a big way, they'll put a frame around me and I'll never be a writer. So I didn't do it. I was 20 years old, and this media hashes people up.

LOTRINGER: And you were doing that while working at the sex-show?

ACKER: I had two-three half-hour shows. And I would have an hour in between each show. So I would go to Tad's Steakhouse and would write, just to keep my mind together otherwise I would have flipped out. I would spend most of my time hanging out in the dressing room with all the other strippers hearing stories. It was the days of a lot of drugs, especially hallucinogens, so the girls just got totally wacked out of their minds and would tell great stories.

②
IDENTITIES

LOTRINGER: Did you write them down?

ACKER: Yeah, but I didn't want to be a sociologist. The stories were very immediate to me so I put everything in the first person, plus some of my dreams.

LOTRINGER: Did you do anything with these stories?

ACKER: After I went to California? Oh I know what happened. David Antin said to me, There's one magazine of prose work that you could publish in that's in the poetry world—Carol Berger's magazine. So I sent her some material and she sent back the usual note, Oh great stuff, lots of energy, send more. So I'm babysitting one night for David and Eleanor Antin and I see this letter on the floor. I see my name so, of course, I read the letter and it's from Carol Berger's saying, This woman is a total nutcase, lock her up in a loony-bin, thinking that these stories were all about me. It was very hard, I was very very sensitive in those days, but I remember being very fascinated that the work had had that kind of power.

LOTRINGER: It was a pretty schitzy experience.

6

ACKER: I became very interested in the model of schizophrenia. I wanted to explore the use of the word I, that's the only thing I wanted to do. So I placed very direct autobiographical, just diary material, right next to fake diary material. I tried to figure out who I wasn't and I went to texts of murderesses. I just changed them into the first person, really not caring if the writing was good or bad, and put the fake first person next to the true first person. And then continue this to see what would happen. I used pre-Freudian texts because I didn't want to deal with Freudian jargon. It was a very naive experiment at first. I was experimenting about identity in terms of language. That's how I started out.

LOTRINGER: But the first person is just a free-for-all word, whoever grabs it becomes it.

ACKER: I also came to the decision that it was a false problem because it's a thing that's made. You create identity, you're not given identity per se. What became more interesting to me wasn't the I, it was text because it's texts that create the identity. That's how I got interested in plagiarism. But that took a few years.

LOTRINGER: What happened during these few years then?

ACKER: I was doing experiments about memory. It was always about how this word I works, what is memory, how does memory and language work, what's the relation between them. I read whoever I could get hold of—Bergson on memory and R.D. Laing/David Cooper.

LOTRINGER: Dissociation as process...

ACKER: Yeah. The idea that you don't need to have a central identity, that a split identity was a more viable way in the world. I was splitting the I into false and true I's and I just wanted to see if this false I was more or less real than the true I; what are the reality levels between false and true and how it worked. And of course there's no difference. By the end of the TARANTULA, when I do the de Sade business, I can't tell what's true or false, except for actual dates. If I say I was born in 1748, I know that's false...

LOTRINGER: Did that happen while you were writing it or afterwards?

ACKER: Afterwards. When you're writing it, your mind is focused on the present, everything's true. And then the next book I did things with repeating texts. If I repeated the same text, would it be the same text? Anyway, that's the early work. And I was playing with other things too. I played with using a lot of horror books, well mainly porn, and putting them in my stories. And writing badly. Basically I was interested in doing everything I wasn't supposed to do. I wrote so many pages a day and that was that. I set up guidelines for each piece, such as you'll use autobiographical and fake autobiographical material, or you're not allowed to rewrite. I really didn't want any creativity. It was task work, and that's how I thought of it.

③

COMMUNITIES

LOTRINGER: The idea of using your imagination to write a story never appealed to you.

ACKER: I hated it really. The word imagination is a bit of a bugaboo. They've used it to place literature on a pedestal.

LOTRINGER: I remember you telling me years ago, I don't have any imagination...

ACKER: I never thought I had imagination. I've never fantasized. I've used other texts, or I've used friends, I've used memories but I've never created stories by making things up.

LOTRINGER: Most writers don't.

ACKER: Yeah, but they always talk about inspiration. I thought there're reasons I'm doing this so I can tell people why I'm doing it and I can talk about the end result. There's nothing mysterious.

LOTRINGER: And what did you do with the end results?

ACKER: I sent the first part of the TARANTULA out and lots of people liked it. It was a time when there was this—there's always been MALE ART, but this was MAIL ART, people mailing things to each other. There was a whole network, and I was part of the network. I sent the first section to about a hundred people and they wrote back to me so I thought, Oh, this is fun. It became a serial novel. The next time I did another six installments, which is NYMPHOMANIACS, there were two hundred of them. We just talked everybody to do it for free. I hustled printers, Peter and I would go and staple them together ourselves, it was a home production industry. I did the last part, THE ADULT LIFE OF TOULOUSE LAUTREC, when I returned to New York. By then too many people wanted them, and I guess I also thought—I didn't think about money in those days—it would be nice to be really published. Anyway that's how it happened. I had this kind of community when I was sending them out which I've never had since .

LOTRINGER: It was a great time. Artists were showing their work to other artists, the outside world wasn't really involved.

ACKER: Yeah, there never was a better time. I met Larry Weiner, Phil Glass was helping out. Lots of people. Women were doing a lot of performance art about identity.

LOTRINGER: Painters were subsidizing the art world.

ACKER: That was it. Sol Lewitt subsidized me, that's what happened. Sol went to Ted Castle and Leandro Katz—Ted is an art-critic and Leandro a filmmaker—and he said he wanted to print these texts as real books. He basically became my patron. I didn't know who Ted and Leandro were—I thought they were part of the St. Mark's Poetry scene—so I came back to New York and lo and behold it wasn't that scene at all. They had a party for my book and Joseph Kosuth and Keith Saulnier were there. I was absolutely flabbergasted cause I'd been reading *Artforum* regularly and worshiped these people. I don't think I could open my mouth the whole evening. From then on I was just in the art world. I hung out at first with Marsha Resnick and Pooh Kaye, people my age. There was Michael McLard and Robin Winters who were solidly artists, and Diego Cortez. Betsy Sussler was part of the group and there was me. I was never an artist.

LOTRINGER: The art world was beginning to open up. Everybody was going to the Mudd Club in White Street. For the first time art was meeting Punk.

A C K E R : It was just before punk, that's when it all started. The community was absolutely strong. Most of my friendships have really come from that time.

L O T R I N G E R : Did the art world reinforce what you were already doing?

A C K E R : I was doing verbally the sort of work that they were doing visually, so it made sense. The language was the same. I could get tons of ideas and I could translate back and forth. I could take stuff.

L O T R I N G E R : What kind of stuff?

A C K E R : I can't remember anything special until it comes to the Metro Pictures times. Then I know that Richard Prince, Sherry Levine and David Salle's work really influenced me. And it's at the end of BLOOD AND GUTS IN HIGH SCHOOL when I start really using plagiarism, with the Genet stuff. So I think that was in the air. You're asking me about direct influences...

L O T R I N G E R : No, I was just wondering how the "translation" works. French theorists use abstractions, but Americans just have a way of looking at objects and reacting to them creatively.

A C K E R : Well, meeting you changed me a lot because by introducing me to the French philosophes, you gave me a way of verbalizing what I had been doing in language. I didn't really understand why I refused to use linear narrative; why my sexual genders kept changing; why basically I am the most disoriented novelist that ever existed. (Laughs). The work of Laing and Cooper, and whoever else I was going to, gave me no way of really understanding why I was writing the way I was writing. I was like a death-dumb-and-blind person for years, I just did what I did but had no way of telling anyone about it, or talking about it. And then when I read ANTI-OEDIPUS and Foucault's work, suddenly I had this whole language at my disposal. I could say, Hi! And that other people were doing the same thing. I remember thinking, Why don't they know me? I know exactly what they're talking about. And I could go farther.

LOTRINGER: Plagiarism, was that something that came out of your exploration of the I?

ACKER: No, the I became a dead issue because I realized that you make the I and what makes the I are texts.

LOTRINGER: But the I never comes on its own. It's always woven in a text .

ACKER: Yeah, but it took me a while to realize that because I am a bit dumb. (Laughs). So I became interested in just text. Other people's texts. If there's no problem with the I, then in terms of text there was no self and other, I could use everyone else's writing. And then it's like a kid; suddenly a toy shop opens up and the toy shop was called culture. Suddenly I thought I didn't even have to pretend I was interested in this problem about identity anymore, I could just bloody copy straight on.

LOTRINGER: Which, of course, you never bloody do.

ACKER: No, I don't. It's very boring, copying, your mind goes. What's fun is what happens when you start playing with a text, it's just like jazz riffs, you go back and forth and down and around. You've got the text in front of you and you go everywhere.

LOTRINGER: That's also what musicians do, lifting stuff.

ACKER: Oh sure. Last night I was talking with a friend about appropriation in music, all these scratched records, and she was saying that her friend Karen Finlay has been ripped off. And I told her: Listen, it's not just that Karen is not getting the money that she should have for her work, I think it's great! I use your work, you use my work, we use everyone's work. I just love that idea, like you can dance...

LOTRINGER: Property is robbery...

ACKER: If I had to be totally honest I would say that what I'm doing is breach of copyright—it's not, because I change words—but so what? We're always playing a game. We earn our money out of the stupid law but we hate it because we know that's a jive. What else can we do? That's one of the basic contradictions of living in capitalism. I sell copyright, that's how I make my money.

LOTRINGER: You sell copyright?

ACKER: That's how writers make their money. Absolutely precisely. The work isn't the property, it's the copyright. Copyright's renewed 26 years twice. I can do anything I want with material that's 52 years old. So what's property? The property dies in 52 years?

LOTRINGER: Didn't you get the rap for breaching copyright in England?

ACKER: What had happened was that a journalist was gunning for me, well that's my opinion. A collection of my earliest work was published in England, and in the section about TOULOUSE LAUTREC there's four pages which I took out of a Harold Robbins novel, a best-selling book called *The Pirate* that had been published some years before. There is a scene there where a rich white woman walks into a disco and picks up a black boy and has sex with him. I changed it to be about Jacqueline Onassis and I entitled the piece "I Want to Be Raped Every Night. Story of a Rich Woman." I think the joke's quite obvious, but the journalist called my publisher and then she called Harold Robbins' publisher, and their response was that, my God, we've got a plagiarist in our midst. So they made a deal that my book would be immediately withdrawn from publication and that I would sign a public apology to Harold Robbins for what I had done. This is not standard literary practice by any means. This in fact is banning. When I heard about this, I said you could do what you want with your edition of the book but I'm certainly not signing a public apology for something I'm not guilty of. I'm not guilty of plagiarism.

LOTRINGER: What do you mean by that?

ACKER: To be guilty of plagiarism, according to the law, is to represent somebody else's material as your material. I haven't done that. I have been very clear that I use other people's material. I haven't quite listed sources in my later books not to sound like an academic, but in many interviews, many theoretical texts, I said where each section came from. I've always told my publishers. There's an introduction to this publication of my early work where I talk about my method of appropriation. I've always talked about it as a literary theory and as a literary method. I haven't certainly hidden anything. Plagiarism is when you actually...

LOTRINGER: ...*pirate* someone else's text! Or rather hijack it, which is the etymology. Hijacking a copyright, no wonder they got upset. Terrorism in literature...

ACKER: What a writer does, in 19th century terms, is that he takes a certain amount of experience and he "represents" that material. What I'm doing is simply taking text to be the same as the world, to be equal to non-text, in fact to be more real than non-text, and start *representing text*. So it's quite clear, I took the Harold Robbins and represented it. I didn't copy it. I didn't say it was mine.

LOTRINGER: You used it as "material," as Heiner Müller did with his Medea. Or reframed it, as Sherry Levine or Richard Prince did with classical photographs.

ACKER: Right, and it seems to me quite a different procedure than the act of plagiarism. I had changed words, I had changed intentionality. Obviously appropriation has been some sort of postmodernist technique in the arts for a number of years, both in the visual arts and in the literary arts, but it's very different cases. It's a legal precedent. The main response from my publisher in England was, Oh Kathy, why are you always making trouble? When I said that to sign this apology was to apologize for twenty years of work, they did not understand. Eventually I did sign the apology, but it was a very specific statement and it was published in all the literary magazines.

LOTRINGER: You said you changed the intentionality of Robbins' text...

ACKER: Robbins is really soft core porn, so I wanted to see what would happen if you changed contexts and just upped the sexuality of the language. It's a simplistic example of deconstruction.

LOTRINGER: I take it you use *deconstruction* in the American sense.

ACKER: Yes, as opposed to construction or reconstruction. You just take other texts and you put them in different contexts to see how they work. You take texts apart and look at the language that's being used, the genre, the kind of sentence structure, there's a lot of contents here that most readers don't see.

LOTRINGER: It's some kind of active reading.

ACKER: I've always loved doing that. Once I saw a James Bond film on TV—this is in the PASOLINI book—and I copied the film, just did a plot summary and Jesus, the most obvious racism was apparent, which you wouldn't really quite think of if you watched the film. I never wanted to be a sociologist, I've always wanted to be present, to write in a way that's most present. The English view of the novel is that there should be irony. Irony is this distance, so you set up a very fine cool style, a very conservative-style way of writing a novel. And I've always hated that. I never wanted that kind of distance.

LOTRINGER: There's not much irony here. I realized that when I published my book, *Overexposed.* I thought that the idea of boring people to death with their own perversions was very funny but everyone took it terribly seriously.

ACKER: You've got to know who your audience is if you're going to do something like that or you run the danger of being misunderstood. Americans are not great at irony. Or it's camp, like Gilbert and George or John Waters' movies, especially the new one.

LOTRINGER: Do you have your readers in mind when you write?

ACKER: No, I'm not writing for the reader.

LOTRINGER: Walter Abish sets up his text like a trap. Everything is carefully calculated to create specific reactions in the reader. You're a total barbarian compared to him. You don't play the game at all.

ACKER: I don't have the reader in mind in that way, I guess because there's no distance. If there's this distance between the reader and the text, the reader's just an observer. I want the reader to come right into the text because that's the only way you can take the journey.

LOTRINGER: So you care for the reader in some way.

ACKER: In some way. You have to. (Laughs). What the reader wants—what the reader's trained to want I should say—is to be at a distance and say, Look at those weird people over there! And I never wanted that "over there."

LOTRINGER: And one of the ways of getting the reader over here is to put yourself here first.

ACKER: I know how to make the reader at least come along on the journey and enter into the text. But the primary pleasure is not for the reader, it's for me. And that's really different from Walter. Probably it makes my texts a bit unreadable.

LOTRINGER: I don't think you would expect your readers to read your novels from beginning to end anyway.

ACKER: No. That might derange friends who'd manage any book from beginning to end, but no, on the whole they can read wherever they want, at least up through DON QUIXOTE. Even in EMPIRE OF THE SENSELESS, which is the most narrative book, you could read pretty much anywhere.

LOTRINGER: Still you have these catch-all nets or structures that keep the whole book together, Dickens, Cervantes...

ACKER: Oh they're structured, they're carefully structured. There's always a beginning and an end. Well, to some of them. GREAT EXPECTATIONS has no beginning nor end, but there's a cumulative effect. I wanted to do some sort of environmental writing, the way Bob Ashley was doing environmental music. I thought that I didn't need a centralized plot or centralized characters, so I would take Dickens and grid him, do a structural analysis, which you know I knew how to do. So I started doing my version of GREAT EXPECTATIONS, cutting it up, not even rewriting,

15

just taking it and putting it together again, like playing with building blocks. I didn't know why the hell I was doing that, but it was fun, it was what I wanted to do. Then when you came along, I had some theory, so that's what I meant by decentralization. There was no centralized structure to any of this and I didn't want there to be.

LOTRINGER: And BLOOD AND GUTS?

ACKER: The English got the end mixed up, and no one noticed, so I guess it's not the most tightly structured book after all. After that it's quite different because I'm not so interested in deconstruction any more. I'm much more interested in narrative.

LOTRINGER: Why did you lose interest in deconstruction?

ACKER: I did that straight through DON QUIXOTE, but then I moved to England and I went in a big circle. I was very much a child of the art world and I had taken it for granted that one worked conceptually. I took a whole bunch of things for granted, especially a premise that's very deep in this society which is that art is separate from politics, and if they joined, politics is always secondary to art. And that's almost needed because this culture is so horrendously moralistic. Under the aegis of art, you're allowed to actually deal with matters of sexuality and other matters of plain old freedom. But what that also does is it keeps the artist from fighting.

LOTRINGER: Unless they are directly threatened, as happened recently with the NEA.

ACKER: They'll fight if censorship comes too close to them, but they won't get out there and say, Hey, this is a political situation and the society's shit. They really just want to get their money and be left alone. In England that's not true at all. England is a very political culture in a way that America isn't. I was shoved up against the wall and asked to explain why I wrote the way I wrote. So I had to come up with the goods. I was forced to grow. I started questioning this sacrosanct position of art maneuvers, of disjunction. I was able to see them in a political context, which I never was before. They have a phrase in England: "Oh, it's terribly arty," and it's a terrible put down. It means you don't care about the community, you don't care about politics. And I must say I'm on the line with one foot in each camp. So I reexamined the whole thing. And suddenly I wasn't so interested in deconstruction, I got sick of doing it. I felt it was terribly easy, which is quite ridiculous cause it wasn't like my work was very accepted.

LOTRINGER: The context was changing too. Expectations weren't so great anymore between Thatcherism and Reagonomics.

ACKER: Yeah. At one point, I thought there was a real need to examine certain things because there was so much hypocrisy. But it really broke down, especially after Watergate. Everybody now knows what's happening. They might not want to see it, but certainly things are very much in the open and you don't have to keep examining everything to see how it works. People know that the CIA has done a lot of chemical warfare testing, they know how things work now; they just don't give a damn. The society's totally disintegrated. We're wallowing in our own fucking nihilism and that's what Baudrillard looks like to me, he wallows in his own nihilism. Not that Baudrillard is apolitical, it's not apolitical at all, but it's a different sort of politics. He's made his point and things have gone on. We're wandering around and we don't know what to do, living in a sort of hell with AIDS and crack and everything else. It always is a guerrilla warfare, so you do have to look at context, the culture, what's happened, to see what makes sense at the moment. By the end of DON QUIXOTE I was doing what I had always done, taking stuff and looking at context, seeing how they worked next to passages that had a lot of political meaning in them and seeing what society meant, but the meaning wasn't clear. And it just wasn't making sense anymore. So I thought I should work toward a reformation of what would be sense. If you scratch hard, you find that I'm a humanist in some weird way. Well, humanist, you know what I mean.

LOTRINGER: You had to start constructing.

ACKER: Construction sounds very positive. People say, Oh, you're not so negative anymore. (Groans). No, I'm not a New Ager. Deconstruction is always a reactive thing and as long as you're dwelling in the reactive you're really reinforcing the society that you hate. So I got very interested with narrative. I started reading a lot of myths. I'm a Westerner with Greek myths, and that's where EMPIRE OF THE SENSELESS begins.

⑤

MAKING MYTH

LOTRINGER: How do you deal with myths in your work? How do you go about making myth, and not just making sense?

ACKER: What I tried to do in EMPIRE OF THE SENSELESS was to start to make a kind of myth that would be applicable to me and my friends.

LOTRINGER: You got interested in the Oedipal myth. Why?

ACKER: Because that's one of the two or three major myths that I was baby-fed. So in EMPIRE OF THE SENSELESS I went to de Sade who, in my mind, is the greatest writer of the Oedipal Myth. Freud and de Sade are the great modern purveyors of that myth, but Sade blasted it wide open. Feminists made me realize then why one would want to decentralize a father, take the father and tear him apart. I had some theory behind it. It also made me realize what my relation to these old authoritarian male poets was. I must have been very influenced by them, but certainly in a perverse way. Charles Olson said that when you write what you have to do is find your own voice, but it all seemed to be very big, almost God-like, and I found this very confusing. I couldn't find my own voice, I didn't know what my own voice was. And I'm sure that's where I started to write in different voices and started to deal with schizophrenia. This was behind it, was in a way a fight against the fathers, because they were very much my fathers. It all fits nicely.

LOTRINGER: Very nicely.

ACKER: I'm not a straightforward feminist, but my interest is in the feminism, that's a change since I left New York. And my best critics are feminists. That's simply where I would locate myself.

LOTRINGER: You used to have problems with women's groups. I remember they were pretty hostile during a tour you made in California.

ACKER: Yeah, but that was a long time ago. I had trouble with the old feminists because of my interest in the nexus of sexuality and politics, and that was anathema to them. That was what I would call the con of equality, the flag that the old feminists were waving, so there was a lot of antagonism. However that's not true now, especially not true of feminism in the United States. I don't have a problem with women's groups anymore. In fact it's the opposite. I'm banned in Germany because of it.

LOTRINGER: Banned?

ACKER: Real censorship. Court verdict. The whole business.

LOTRINGER: Did the court realize that your stuff has been lifted from books that aren't banned...

ACKER: In this court verdict they wrote down the plot of BLOOD AND GUTS and the poor guy couldn't even figure out what the plot was. So they banned me for three reasons and one of the reasons is experimentality...

LOTRINGER: Experimentality was the major accusation?

ACKER: No. First there was kindersex...

LOTRINGER: Ah ah.

ACKER: Which is great. I kept wondering where's kindersex in the novel at first. That's between Janey and her father. They didn't get it that it was a double play. They thought it was real. They took everything absolutely literally. Janey has sex with her father, that's kindersex. Then there's S/M, which is probably the most correct thing they came up with. Yes, there's S/M in the book. And then there's experimentality. So they got a precis of the plot and when they came to the Persian poems...

LOTRINGER: What did they do with that?

ACKER: They didn't know what to do obviously. You read this court verdict and it's like, Get it out of here! Just don't want this thing! Then they investigated me and found out I had worked as a stripper and said, Though she's well-known to be interested in the Women's Question, she doesn't discuss the Women's Question enough and she's worked as a stripper.

LOTRINGER: And working as a stripper, that's not working at the Woman's Question?

ACKER: God!

LOTRINGER: Well, I know for a fact that you're totally different from what you write.

ACKER: Well, it's a big question. For the writing I don't have a problem, but it's a problem personally. In England it was absolutely horrible. The media had made this huge image of Kathy Acker. It was a problem with friendship, the media image is so much this kind of sexual image. I'm very well-known there and I get tons of work, but to say that they like what I do, no, I wouldn't say that. They fetishize what I do.

LOTRINGER: It's something you obviously play with.

ACKER: Of course.

LOTRINGER: But you wouldn't expect them to take it so literally.

ACKER: Oh it was pretty absurd there. At a certain point it's hard to play with it. You can't say anything to them, you just giggle. (Pause). Most people think I'm much harder than I am.

LOTRINGER: It's all part of the Black Tarantula syndrome. One way of making your work legitimate, I guess, is to work it through your persona. If you are not the I, but the I becomes you, then you have to offer it as some kind of performance.

ACKER: Yeah, I think that's very precise. So it's like an actress, I act through the novels.

LOTRINGER: And beside the novels too.

ACKER: When I'm writing I become the characters in the novel, but the characters in the novel aren't me. People always think they're me, and it's a drag.

LOTRINGER: That's what happens to dealers of myths. They become myth. Now you don't even need to be a real poete maudit, all you need is—what? Tattoos on your body...

ACKER: That's what tattooing is for me, it's myth.

LOTRINGER: You seem to become more and more myth. Each time we meet I see more tattoos cropping up on you. You must have been very busy. Are you going to have them on both shoulders and in the back?

ACKER: No, I'm not going to have them on that shoulder. I'll leave the shoulders as is for the moment. I'm going to have these come down diagonally on the back. It's been growing for two years (Laughs). I'm now getting these tribal things.

LOTRINGER: Genet or Artaud had a saving grace, they dealt with the sacred. There's always elements of ritual in myth-making.

ACKER: Well, I have the body. I am very much a primitive if you scratch me.

LOTRINGER: But it's all on the surface. It's like myth-making, the body takes the place of the I.

ACKER: Yeah, because the body's more text. When I first saw tattooing, I thought it was the most fabulous artwork because it was so direct, it was on someone's body. And to ask some artist to do their artwork on your body... What trust! Jesus, that's incredible art.

LOTRINGER: You don't even have to transfer anything to the writing anymore. The body is it.

ACKER: Tattoo means writing. It's how they used to write in Tahiti.

LOTRINGER: So you got written.

ACKER: Yeah. Someone wrote on me, which is pretty incredible. It's all the process of making. I invented someone to help me make my body. And I had to trust that person, I have to believe I like his artwork.

LOTRINGER: It's there to stay.

ACKER: They always do it in ink on me before—they can erase it, so you're not taking a huge amount of chance. In my new novel, the male character is Japanese and he was trained in Ukeo (the 19th century wood-cutting style) by his master Yoshi Toshi. He came to this country and what he really wanted to do was transfer the art and become a tattooist. He wants to do the perfect tattoo. One day a young girl comes to his studio and he knows she's the one he has to tattoo, so he drugs her, but she doesn't live through the tattoo, she dies from it. He wants to escape but she comes back to him as a ghost and they have a night of very hot sex in a graveyard. Then he's free to go. The myth's about how a person becomes a hero and it's based on the development of Prince Genji.

LOTRINGER: Tattoo has worked its way into your writing. You told me that now you're doing bodybuilding.

ACKER: Right now I train five times a day with a trainer. I could train for competition if I wanted to, which I don't. This is as serious as I ever got and I love it. I really love it. It's teaching me a lot about writing.

LOTRINGER: How?

ACKER: Because it's about focusing and about consciousness. People assume writing is cerebral whereas body-building is material. But they work together, and how they work together I'm fascinated by. It's only Mishima that's really talked about it. When you work legs there's a certain curl that's very painful to do and as a body-builder you have to learn to get through pain, or rather learn to live through it. You can't do it otherwise. So where your mind goes when your body feels these various things and how the mind works with the body, is really interesting, at least to me.

LOTRINGER: It's about control?

ACKER: The body's so rich, who's controlling it? It's like text. When you write, are you controlling a text? When you're really writing you're not, you're fucking with it. And I'd say the same thing with body-building when you're going through that pain. What you do, when you body-build, is work to failure. You put a

22

frame around specific muscle-groups and you work each group to failure. Actually I want to work past failure, which is negative work. And I think you're doing exactly the same thing with the text .

LOTRINGER: What's past-failure for a text?

ACKER: To go into the space of wonder. What I have always hated about the bourgeois story is that it closes down. I don't use the bourgeois story-line because the real content of that novel is the property structure of reality. It's about ownership. That isn't my world-reality. My world isn't about ownership. In my world people don't even remember their names, they aren't sure of their sexuality, they aren't sure if they can define their genders. That's the way you feel in the mythical stories. You don't know quite why they act the way they act, and they don't care.

LOTRINGER: There's no psychology or development.

ACKER: The reader doesn't own the character. There's a lot of power in narrative, not in story. It gives me the chance to use that form of power without having to know in advance what I'm going to write. That's what I meant by primitive: you don't quite know what the world is, you're in a strange world. The early Greek stories were all about strange worlds. Even in classical Greek drama, there were the known rules of the city—in Antigone you have the king—but it's all about fate and fate is unknown. And I like that landscape much better. You're allowed to just move, you're allowed to wander. It's like travelling. I've always envied men this and I can never travel being a woman. I always wanted to be a sailor, that's really what I love.

LOTRINGER: When you returned to San Francisco six or seven years ago you planned to go sailing around the world. I remember a postcard I received then. You were very excited about it.

ACKER: Yeah, but we didn't know how to sail... I guess I just want to go on a journey and so I start with a sentence and then the language twists and turns and you don't even remember where you've been, you're always faced with the present. You're always going somewhere, you always end up somewhere. You want to be surprised. That's what I like, all writers like. To have that sense of wonder.

LOTRINGER: So you're not deconstructing anymore, even the Oedipal Myth. You're trying to build... something.

ACKER: Yeah, and that's what I'm really interested in. EMPIRE OF THE SENSELESS was still the old stuff, but there was a narrative there. IN MEMORIAM TO IDENTITY is much more that. I still plagiarize, but it's cleaned up so that the primitive narrative is coming through more strongly.

LOTRINGER: Why do you have to use other texts for that?

ACKER: I have to use other texts when I write, that's just how am, but now I don't have irony towards them. The irony is gone. I'm not so interested in pulling them apart, I don't have that suspicion toward them any more, cause I respect them. I want to learn from them about myth because they're both myth-dealers.

LOTRINGER: And what myths are you dealing with?

ACKER: What I'm really interested in is this myth of romantic love. This is what IN MEMORIAM is about. Rimbaud I also took as one of the first major poetic myths for us. If you think of our idea of the poet, it would be Rimbaud.

LOTRINGER: And the new book?

ACKER: The new book I couldn't name the myth. It's almost new. I'm at this place where I was prior to when I met you where don't have the theory anymore to talk about it.

New York, October 1989–May 1990.

POLITICS

(MY FIRST WORK, WRITTEN WHEN 21 YEARS OLD)

the filthy bedcover on stage I'm allergic to this way of life mine?
the last time I got on stage for the first ten minutes I felt I wasn't
me I was going through mechanical personality changes and
actions I got scared I might flip in front of the sex-crazy lunatics
finally got into the Santa Claus routine I was a little girl all excited
because Santa Claus was going to bring me Christmas presents I
couldn't go to sleep I was waiting and waiting and then and then
you know what happened doctor Santa Claus came right into my
room I'm taking my clothes my shoes off rubbing my breasts
Lenny dreamt last night about fucking Cyrelle she was lecturing
him on how to fuck a woman he told her that he didn't need the
lecture she thought he was wrong he was sucking an older
woman's cunt it was also a cock without changing from a cunt
this is a romantic section a very romantic life ha ha I was writing
in the projection room the shits said they'd clean and wax the
floor it's still piss black can't see no roaches no more it's hotter
than usual the projectionist was constantly bugging me some guy
they say drunk hit Josie on her ass during her show yesterday his
hat the cashier says he came up told him you're not allowed to
bring liquor up here then the cashier an Indian guy turns to
Washington an old black janitor tells him that he's not to come
again on the weekends he has no mind he can't remember anything he's not to ask to get paid again he gets $1.00 he's too old
he won't be able to work much longer he's sick he's senile he's
looking at me red blearing eyes we're at the Embers cruddy food
at least no one's taking off his clothes they all want to SCREW
this week (we find in the projection room) is about orgies men-
tions every place but ours only the fuzz know about 113 swingers
SCREW says are very jealous about their mates? you can't get
involved with a girl you fuck at an orgy unless you've got her
guy's O.K. which isn't they say likely I don't know about vice-

versa at an orgy everyone wants to have everyone else only once no two guys together the males want to watch the females screw so that occurs it turns them on the best orgy I ever went to a cunt's writing started with two girls making it on the livingroom floor Lenny tells me Lawrence is a romantic Kangaroo red and black striped overalls no hair I don't know what the fuck to do with it I'm getting to look so ugly it won't do anything like stand straight out fuzz into balls two more shows and everything's over I felt dead writing before I could be dead now waking up I got a sacred Mexican ring yesterday to do just that remember every single dream for the next two weeks as soon as I wake up not getting so pissed off all the time completely hostile I'd like Jewels this life's not romantic enough too hidden yet to be found in the fucking brain and mind I have to get back to the show Lenny's putting on his coat son of a bitch

after we had dinner at this god awful chinese restaurant fake chinese gardens the waiter shit wouldn't give another bowl to us for the winter melon soup for two on the menu Mickey was barely able to kiss Mark goodbye we went to Mark's house 13th and A stories about how If you venture out there after dark one block or more you automatically get raped mugged castrated we smoked went into the bedroom to see the new waterbed it was gorgeous like being in the ocean the waves lapping back and forth it was the only thing in the room except for a tape deck white walls no curtains Mark said he was going to paint the walls different shades of blue striped in a funnel the rug would be dyed to match the ceiling the floor would be an actual funnel you'd go right through I was completely smashed Mark was hot for Lenny spent an hour? two hours? making these absurd hints he only wanted to sleep with Ellen the new dancer Lenny was playing dumb too smashed or not digging he finally said do you want to sleep with me Lenny didn't want me to leave the room I didn't want to leave the waterbed under any circumstances my dress kept getting undone earlier in the evening Mark had been kissing me he gave a speech about male male fucking god knows why he ever wants a female I said I the fucking cats didn't want to sleep with Mark Mark said he'd prefer Lenny between the two of us he'd take us both he didn't think I was ugly I was so complimented I didn't want to watch watching Lenny fuck someone and not being able to be involved wanting to would blow me Mark kept pushing Lenny telling me to go into the livingroom Lenny didn't want me there Ronny came in bill blass jumpsuit blue with a thin white belt Bill Blass scarf my my richies Hanky Panky crackers from Boston I ate one and didn't like it Mark wanted to go back to the livingroom I wanted to get out of there back to the cats I prefer gay guys because I'm not under pressure constantly to fuck them watch if my clothing's always closed which it's not I was feeling anomalous Mark started saying the mattress in the waterbed on the waterbed is torn I have to fix it he even threaded a real needle Lenny can you help me Ronny's cracking ridiculous jokes Mark's done it so often he even has it timed Mark says you can watch Ronny's not a voyeur we watch Rat-Race Debbie Schmereynolds an incredibly creepy flic in which Debbie's a good girl who'd rather give up her guy than prostitute I don't remember if she's living with him in sin it was very romantic Ronny and I were finally talking Johnny Carson turned on crude gags about hookers drag queens everyone's one for fun I'm learning about Middle America the whole place is mad I'm cold to Lenny don't admit I am which is nasty I want to see my cats Mark has one Tiffany she's seven weeks pregnant and crawls through almost closed windows and bars no one else comes it was a party not even Mickey Mark said that Mickey would be very upset if he knew that Mark slept with anyone else Mark would if Mickey did it's quite nutty there's this rich guy Jack who's been supporting Mark still is? they have an expensive looking place not much furniture yet no books of course we're open for any garbage I get pissed off when Mark kisses me and calls me a girl he's upset I am I try to relax rub him goodnight Lenny's acting like he's lost his mind we get a ride with this dope seller creep doesn't know why anyone would live in a commune not enough money to the 8th street subway this is the first dream sequence 1:17 I have to go out for the rest of the day get my hair cut again thank god

last night with Mary was a complete failure I couldn't understand what she was saying I've never seen any Warhol films I felt she was deaf was I supposed to fuck her Harriet's work was gorgeous eccentric Beardsley one interpretation could be that I was maniacal and Mary was uptight me babbling I could be far from reality I don't know no one is willing to come close enough to tell me why the fuck should they I wouldn't be my ugly self Mary might have been very shy and into herself I got smashed and watched T.V. was she smashed she said so at one point I don't know when anyone's putting me on anymore lying to me Melvin wrote me he can't live with Wilma with any girl? anyone? for any length of time my basic problem is I can't quite believe anything and can't

react to anything similarly I never react to things when they happen but only later when they're less threatening Jeffrey's probably dying Seeley unable to be political which was his life for the
past four years when Melvin was here at Christmas he wanted to
sleep with us I told Lenny no before when Lenny asked me Lenny
said yee—h I personally had been avoiding sleeping with him for
the past year they went into the bedroom 2:00 in the morning
bloody cold I smoked half an ounce of pot couldn't get high it was
shitting cold Lenny wanted to go to sleep kept bitching at me to
get into the fucking bed I took off my bluejeans finally had a thick
black and white diamond bodystocking on under it and sat on the
bed between their legs I tried to think about how warm they
were in the bed not me I couldn't adjust to coldly stripping fucking Melvin the first time we'd been too close we kept wondering
if we should sleep in other beds various arrangements Susie
Rosenberg about 6:00 I managed to get in and take the rest of my
clothes off you wouldn't know I did it for a living we were going
to play ghost for the next week Melvin acted like a complete shit
we saw him once more he was going to sleep with us brought us
free food he'd call up Mary we'd all go to Mary's Lenny was feeling shitty working all day Melvin had his father's car so we didn't
have to take the subway he decided to stay at Mary's we bitched
Lenny was dead tired he gave us a ride home free radio Melvin
isn't even that good in bed very rough Mary doesn't like his cock
he's going nuts about Jeffrey told us later I finally agreed to
speak with him on the telephone he had gone back to Mary's had
a fight with her about going to 3000 parties Mary said that he
came over on New Year's Eve three days later acted abominably
god knows I feel closer to him today Bob calls up I have to work
tonight the new couple fucked maybe tomorrow night he doesn't
know he's sooo busy maybe I won't be able to train another couple in time hah ten easy steps to Hollywood bare the vagina
destroy yourself he couldn't be bothered a couple of nights' work
he makes me puke I can't work in such hell I call up Mark at his
house he'll do the show whenever I want nights (he works days) I
need Bob's crap like a hole in my head soon I can get back to
sleep Bob was blabbing about my using someone else would they
know what to do of course how to simulate repulsion more money
for his fat gullet Lenny didn't leave me some dead tired Bob is
disgusting a destroyer of human minds the second dream
sequence written at 11:40 I'm feeling like shit get along with
Hannah (I am) I can't cite down peacocks my nightmares all these
invulnerable thoughts my great beauty I can try to talk to Hannah

third dream tomorrow tell her Lenny says she's scared I should do everything to help her relax I want to be alone Greta Garbo Scylla and Charibdis I don't know how to return

I was a young wife last night I was scared that my husband took drugs you smoke a pot cold to sex unless I danced alone knowing that there were fifty other men in the red hotel room I got really hot he kept taking too long blew him he ate me the usual we still had time left so I danced naked Ike and Tina Turner's RESPECT he yelled at me to get on the floor in the doggie position I did immediately got up he said do it you're supposed to do whatever I say I did it looked up at him and went rrrf-rrf rrrf-rrf the shits broke up I started crying again I want to go home to mommy you stupid cunt I want to see my mommy you're a brute I don't want to be married to you any longer O.K. we'll go see your mother I like her too Mark's good at being aggressive a tinge of nastiness they're sadists a good fit I worked easily except for the sex I felt weird with Mark couldn't get into it and fake coming I was more interested in kissing him or looking at his body during the intermission I was talking to Ellen Mark and Mickey were making up she had done tricks for a while three times once a week went up to George Raft's hotel room he had an old-young travelling companion she fucked the companion turning Raft's sex the whole night Raft was nice to her she says told her that she should tell each guy she deals with why should you pay the pimp? agency? I don't remember anything pay me and I'll take the price down $10. she should also pick two or three guys she trusts to be nice and pay have them as private clientele not deal with strangers she was in a precarious position might get arrested beaten too large a cock and couldn't refuse alone in the room he knew one guy who got off on lying in a coffin and seeing the girl freak out Mark comes up says that he thinks that no one if he didn't feel restrained would be normal weird ways of getting off Lizzy's licking Paul's ears his neck they're fighting with the ball hanging from the scratching post and kissing each other one girl he got so hepped up by his half lying said that she really wanted to blow a guy just as he was about to come for him to ejaculate over her face so she could rub it in a typical porno movie ending Mark repeated to her what she had said it was in a room of people she got uptight immediately left the room I didn't have any trouble getting home Mark and Mickey walked me to the subway station so I could see if anyone was following me the D train came fast the AA I thought two guys were following me up 163rd but nothing happened Lenny and Hannah were asleep I hope Hannah's O.K. she's strangely quiet and in her room she might have killed herself she just got up I have to speak to her she's cold blaaah naah I was still jumpy wanted to rest eat some bread Lenny had woken up for a sec too conked out I tried to get Melvin worried by his letter the telephone was coocoo crawled into bed with Lenny but couldn't get to sleep for a few hours this is the third dream sequence I'm not going to do anything for the next two days put down my actual dream an affair between me Mark and Lenny in the middle of the morning the joke about the rubbers: my daddy told me never to do it without a rubber whatever that is what are you talking about it's not raining the roof of the hotel room was leaking onto the gold bed long blonde fluffy hair over my cunt

Lenny won't call me La Mort he says he doesn't want to say a name that strange I dig the pun the whole day's been like this: we can't do the old show can't do any show except one which means something to us beyond the bread we make we probably should quit this fucking job the 12:30 show's gone a fuzz appeared about 12:05 saying that the theater couldn't open until 12:30 the shits make up their own rules anything they crave syphilis wet cunt crap cock puss I Lenny says he'll call me the german for murder murderer? Morda that's better it'll be romantic I won't mind doing the show which is a really shitty show today but with the creeps males chauvinists rednecks pukes John Birchers worse liberals murderers we get in the audience it's a strong show they don't want to see anything but dead cunt they make everything dead with their eyes they're not going to dig any jokes they haven't for three months I come out dance strip do hard spreads no expression 10 seconds each held still to Ike and Tina Turner's RESPECT dance at the end sadism hands on the hip as they clap Lenny's the Shit Boss Mister Wolf call me Wolf that's real I have to fuck him to get the job dancing in his theater my boyfriend's been busted etc. at the end I get the job of course we have to write a better 10-minute conversation about job Bob Wolf I hate giving these fuckers spreads opening myself but we have to do the truth we might as well begin acting that way our romanticism a guy comes over here to use the sugar I jump Lenny asks if I got scared I'm always scared whenever now strange guys come over to talk to me we see Mark and Mickey in the afternoon in the middle of the third show I say there's a friend of mine hello the only line the audience digs they're tripping more tea in my cup Mark stares at the stage lights my yellow socks and red and blue shoes I have to talk to Lenny the Embers again confusion we have to speak loud and very distinctly because the lines are symbols real there ain't no conversation O.K. the audience digs the sadism bastards pimps every male's a pimp in this cruddy society caters to his lousy moneyed disease you get fed it from birth and can't get away except by severe disruption I'm a pervert a sneak I dig buying clothes nothing else the harder the cut the better I get confused about what people expect me to do I'm talking French today an Italian waiter asks me what I'm writing I start answering him in French Lenny says he's good-looking I agree in my head but not turned on I never am I sound like I'm in the 50's not here on 42nd street I like people who say things I haven't heard before that's shit Mark was saying that he hates earning money he has to figure out how to maintain it living he's scared to walk around in the streets with money anymore he gives it to Mickey great solution Mickey's laughing so hard he looks like he's an epileptic Mark's calling him she which is true they're getting deeper and deeper Mark wants to know if he's talking too loud he tries to be silent and actually is seven minutes he felt bad watching me on the stage all the shits cared about was my cunt they moved as I moved so they wouldn't miss a glimpse light meat they can't now he can't be around 42nd street he wants the bread to furnish his apartment acid doesn't last forever 100 tabs a day and an empty forest he'd be happy forever: the paradise I eat raw fish and chicken Lenny tempura and fish with soy sauce and ginger it's worth $13. half a dirty show the waitresses won't go near Mark and Mickey who are giggling like babies wanting to touch each other Mark says he likes Kali's dancing the best he'd like to work with her only she isn't as good with the audience as I am I feel hurt like the guy who told Lenny he didn't like my body then saw me sitting behind and ran like a frightened rat Mark's bluntness makes me easy around him I wouldn't commit myself to him in some dream or reality caused by a dream he and Mickey start saying that a woman should be subservient to a man it's only in America that women lead can lead the men around Mark's not a man he's not involved after chopping wood all day in the forest the man throws open the door of the cabin yells where's my dinner the woman cowers rushes to get it the vegetables not cooked right he throws her against the door we're all getting into it the restaurant's aghast take your clothes off wash my feet warm the shitting bed he'll throw her to the dogs howling in the darkness just beyond the closed door Mark says that if we took the bed offstage and substituted the low Japanese table Lenny could eat me with chopsticks *oriental dish*

I had been taking trains back and forth I had taken the wrong train past 159th street in the Bronx? into country and had to get back it was only possible by transferring twice one stop at Columbia a library beautiful green and old red and white stones the bus passed by the steps along a narrow street I could get stuck there I got out at a department store six floors high I saw something I wanted then secondhand leather culottes very narrow until the hips where there was an exaggerated flare wider than a skirt hem for each leg with a thick band of green elastic around the bottom a saleswoman was showing another customer how stretchable the legs were I went up to the sixth floor to find the clothes there was a huge center room small rooms around it some contained colored fish tanks some were boutiques there were these skimpy dresses in one boutique elastic provided a thick waist tweed flowing lines very short surprisingly close-fit I tried a skirt on kept trying to find the culottes but I couldn't the clothes might have been too expensive Lenny was urging me to go saying what I already knew the last bus would leave at any minute I'd never be able to return I was going crazy wanting to get something before I couldn't anymore the culottes were missing we were just about to leave I was cold knew that I should get up to put something on I heard the door fumbling I had locked it from the inside scared that Hannah couldn't get in I opened it this woman came in slowly a large smile a Japanese face I couldn't back up she could have had a gun she looked a bit like Hannah a bright yellow and red I didn't see the other colors horizontal stripes a wide-knit dress to the floor she kept coming almost gliding forward her smile was terrifying there might have been a gun in her hand she might be robbing me wanting to kill me I am aware I can't get away I knew these girls who were whores old college friends they were being shoved around by their pimp I was doing similar work but not as bad it was a grey-brown street similarly colored air the beginning of night their flesh was thick white and sick-looking I noticed it had become that way since they started doing that work one girl huge buttocks in blue stretch pants said to the others that she had gotten a job being a maid she couldn't wait she could be alone with him the other two said she should watch out she might get in trouble they were being brainwashed by Bob Wolf I went into my door a few steps away I'm on a train something prostitution Bob Wolf one lean blonde woman about my age I also used to know her at Brandeis is telling two young girls one lying down with a heavy dark blue knit thing over her stomach how to be hippies or revolutionaries they have to break off all ties learn not to want lots of money I'm almost equal to her but not yet one girl says she has angus there's a murder one hepatitis she's the sickest it seems one with colitis I tell the one with colitis that if she really had colitis she'd be screaming in pain I've had it she has to have something else maybe a spastic colon they're all infectious diseases they might get each other sicker they were also connected to Bob Wolf prostitution it wasn't so upsetting since they could still think were becoming revolutionaries the train was moving out of there before that I had to get through a snow tunnel Elizabeth was a male was going down I was in a room wanted to make this guy much younger than me his mother was coming Bernie whom I had actually known almost slept with a student of mine in San Diego Mark and Mickey trying to touch each other a huge reddish cock standing upright I wanted to watch also touch I wasn't a homosexual and couldn't fit in

had to go to work yesterday Josie's boyfriend Ralph got busted by the feds they broke down the door ripped the apartment apart T.V. bed furniture they arrested everyone in the place then waited for a few hours arresting everyone who buzzed the bell Ralph tried to escape so they shot him in the arm no one fixed his wound when he got to prison so he would have died if it hadn't been for the inmates $10,000. bail $5,000. had to be raised in cash. Josie had $1500. in the bank the feds took her bankbook so she couldn't get at the dough they didn't find the $2,000. hidden in the stove she's been going coocoo trying to raise the rest of the dough before they kick Ralph off he's going to skip ball as soon as he can he's been arrested too many times before she was going to prostitute Marty was in the theater she told him Ralph had been busted what could she do to raise bail she'd do anything Marty said what for drugs? I'm not going to do shit for no drug dealer I don't want no drugs in this theater he's not a drug dealer he's a psychedelic love-freak dealer Ken had told us on Christmas Marty gave him his $100. coke-snorters as presents Josie comes in every day sunk on barbiturates higher on dope Mark and Mickey are arguing Mark's pissed off he can't freely pick up any-one he wants to mainly guys some guy says to Mickey bye Mick Mark blows a gut how dare you talk to someone tell him your name you have no right to talk to anyone about our problems don't get the actors uptight blah blah he can't do the show anymore he wants us to do all of the work dance for 15 minutes seduce him when he comes on stage don't say a word god forbid he should have to think of a joke to crack I'm not going to take that kind of shit he makes the same money I do I tell him get someone else to do the show Ellen and I switch which isn't fair to Ellen but she takes shit all the time I get back for the 2:30 show Bob Wolf Big Shit Boss is standing in the back his hair's down to his shoulders to show that he's a hippy and loves everyone he wants to speak to me in an ominous tone I tell Mark start first what the fuck do you mean by almost quitting you can't walk out on a show I won't take that sort of crap I tell him very slowly controlling myself as much as possible to talk and not just to hit him I hate his guts so much the first and second shows on Sunday there's broken glass in the bed it's raining through the roof on the floor where I have to dance and on the bed so I'm working all day in sopping wet clothes and I'm overheated the rug's torn where I dance I keep tripping almost breaking my neck there's no music the place stinks the bedspread's turned brown it's so fucking filthy he starts screaming at me what right do you have to quit you just get out I don't need you you can't get out whenever you please I've tripled audiences on Sundays we've paid you we've never done nothing to you I'm going to quit unless you fix that stage up in two weeks I'm not taking shit you've got my two weeks' notice get the hell out just give me notice get the hell out who are you to threaten me I'm not threatening you I'm telling you point-blank clean this turd fuck shit up Reggie came over last night he and Lenny were going to work for a few hours then we'd all eat dinner I got some wine and cheese for the moment Lenny was sitting on Reggie's lap kissing him they went into the bedroom Lenny told me Reggie said he didn't want to be alone with Lenny anymore Lenny called me could I come into the bedroom I had to peel vegetables but it could wait Lenny was reading a Paul Bowles' story a guy is hot for his son finds out his son's homo and blows a gasket they both go off to Havana I was lying beside Reggie smelling his skin and barely touching him I got into it really hot so I got up to go to the kitchen masturbate in a little privacy they all came in why'd you get up so I told Lenny I was hot for Reggie so Lenny wouldn't think I was bored with his reading Reggie seemed hurt I was talking in a low voice to Lenny I explained he acted nice kissed me we were in bed Reggie fucking me much you have to become a criminal or a pervert I'm in the bathtub touching the bones in my face I have no idea what I feel like I never touch myself except for occasionally masturbating a few times stick a finger up my asshole or lick my nipple I draw my fingers around the back of my neck I want to shave my hair off again toes knees I admire criminals in my head knowing they're shits businessmen motherfuckers like everyone else I don't want to fuck it doesn't mean what it should no one else thinks like this anymore I say angelic I'm sick of fucking not knowing who I am

NEW YORK CITY IN 1979

—Well, my man's gonna get me out of here as soon as he can.

—When's that gonna be, honey?

—So what? Your man pays so he can put you back on the street as soon as possible.

—Well, what if he wants me back on the street? That's where I belong. I make him good money, don't I? He knows that I'm a good girl.

—Your man ain't anything! Johnny says that if I don't work my ass off for him, he's not going to let me back in the house.

—I have to earn two hundred before I can go back.

—Two hundred? That ain't shit! You can earn two hundred in less than a night. I have to earn four hundred or I might just as well forget sleeping, and there's no running away from Him. My baby is the toughest there is.

—Well, shit girl, if I don't come back with eight hundred I get my ass whupped off.

—That's cause you're junk.

—I ain't no stiff! All of you are junkies. I know what you do!

—What's the matter, honey?

—You've been sitting on that thing for an hour.

—The pains are getting bad. OOgh. I've been bleeding two days now.

—OOgh OOgh OOgh.

—She's gonna bang her head off. She needs a shot.

—Tie a sweater around her head. She's gonna break her head open.

—You should see a doctor, honey.

—The doctor told me I'm having an abortion.

—Matron. Goddamnit. Get your ass over here matron!

—I haven't been bleeding this bad. Maybe this is the real abortion.

—Matron! This little girl is having an abortion! You do something. Where the hell is that asshole woman? (The matron throws an open piece of Kotex to the girl.) The service here is getting worse and worse!

—You're not in a hotel. honey.

—It used to be better than this. There's not even any goddamn food. This place is definitely going downhill.

—Oh, shutup. I'm trying to sleep. I need my sleep, unlike you girls, cause I'm going back to work tomorrow.

—Now what the hell do you need sleep for? This is a party. You sleep on your job.

—I sure know this is the only time I get any rest. Tomorrow it's back on the street again.

—If we're lucky.

LESBIANS are women who prefer their own ways to male ways.

LESBIANS prefer the convoluting halls of sensuality to direct goal-pursuing mores.

LESBIANS have made a small world deep within and separated from the world. What has usually been called the world is the male world.

Convoluting halls of sensuality lead to depend on illusions. Lies and silence are realer than truth.

Either you're in love with someone or you're not. The one thing about being in love with someone is you know you're in love: You're either flying or you're about to kill yourself.

I don't know anyone I'm in love with or I don't know if I'm in love. I have all these memories. I remember that as soon as I've gotten fucked, like a dog I no longer care about the man who just fucked me who I was madly in love with.

So why should I spend a hundred dollars to fly to Toronto to get laid by someone I don't know if I love I don't know if I can love I'm an abortion? I mean a hundred dollars and once I get laid I'll be in agony: I won't be doing exactly what I want. I can't live normally i.e. with love so: there is no more life.

The world is gray afterbirth. Fake. All of New York City is fake is going to go all my friends are going crazy all my friends know they're going crazy disaster is the only thing that's happening.

Suddenly these outbursts in the fake, cause they're so open, spawn a new growth. I'm waiting to see this growth.

I want more and more horrible disaster in New York cause I desperately want to see that new thing that is going to happen this year.

JANEY is a woman who has sexually hurt and been sexually hurt so much she's now frigid.

She doesn't want to see her husband anymore. There's nothing between them.

Her husband agrees with her that there's nothing more between them.

But there's no such thing as nothingness. Not here. Only death whatever that is is nothing. All the ways people are talking to her now mean nothing. She doesn't want to speak words that are meaningless.

Janey doesn't want to see her husband again.

The quality of life in this city stinks. Is almost nothing. Most people now are deaf-mutes only inside they're screaming. BLOOD. A lot of blood inside is going to fall. MORE and MORE because inside is outside.

New York City will become alive again when the people begin to speak to each other again not information but real emotion. A grave is spreading its legs and BEGGING FOR LOVE.

Robert, Janey's husband, is almost a zombie.

He walks talks plays his saxophone pays for groceries almost like every other human. There's no past. The last six years didn't exist. Janey hates him. He made her a hole. He blasted into her. He has no feeling. The light blue eyes he gave her; the gentle hands; the adoration: AREN'T. NO CRIME. NO BLOOD. THE NEW CITY. Like in Fritz Lang's METROPOLIS.

This year suffering has so blasted all feelings out of her she's become like a person. Janey believes it's necessary to blast open her mind constantly and destroy EVERY PARTICLE OF MEMORY THAT SHE LIKES.

A sleeveless black T-shirt binds Janey's breasts. Pleated black fake-leather pants hide her cocklessness. A thin leopard tie winds around her neck. One gold-plated watch, the only remembrance of the dead mother, binds one wrist. A thin black leather band binds the other. The head is almost shaved. Two round prescription mirrors mask the eyes.

Johnny is a man who don't want to be living so he doesn't appear to be a man. All his life everyone wanted him to be something. His Jewish mother wanted him to be famous so he wouldn't live the life she was living. The two main girlfriends he has had wanted him to support them in the manner to which they certainly weren't accustomed even though he couldn't put his flabby hands on a penny. His father wanted him to shut up.

All Johnny wants to do is make music. He wants to keep everyone and everything who takes him away from his music off him. Since he can't afford human contact, he can't afford desire. Therefore he hangs around with rich zombies who never have anything to do with feelings. This is a typical New York artist attitude.

New York City is a pit-hole: Since the United States government, having decided that New York City is no longer part of the United States of America, is dumping all the laws the rich people want such as anti-rent-control laws and all the people they don't want (artists, poor minorities, and the media in general) on the city and refusing the city Federal funds; the American bourgeoisie has left. Only the poor: artists, Puerto Ricans who can't afford to move... and rich Europeans who fleeing the terrorists don't give a shit about New York... inhabit this city.

Meanwhile the temperature is getting hotter and hotter so no one can think clearly. No one perceives. No one cares. Insane madness come out like life is a terrific party.

IN FRONT OF THE MUDD CLUB, 77 WHITE STREET

Two rich couples drop out of a limousine. The women are wearing outfits the poor people who were in ten years ago wore ten years ago. The men are just neutral. All the poor people who're making this club fashionable so the rich want to hang out here, even though the poor still never make a buck off the rich pleasure, are sitting on cars, watching the rich people walk up to the club.

Some creeps around the club's entrance." An open-shirted skinny guy who says he's just an artist is choosing who he'll let into the club. Since it's 3:30 A.M. there aren't many creeps. The artist won't let the rich hippies into the club.

> —Look at that car.
> —Jesus. It's those rich hippies' car.
> —Let's take it.
> —That's the chauffeur over there.

—Let's kidnap him.

—Let's knock him over the head with a bottle.

—I don't want no terrorism. I wanna go for a ride.

—That's right. We've got nothing to do with terrorism. We'll just explain we want to borrow the car for an hour.

—Maybe he'll lend us the car if we explain we're terrorists-in-training. We want to use that car to try out terrorist tricks.

After 45 minutes the rich people climb back into their limousine and their chauffeur drives them away.

A girl who has gobs of brown hair like the foam on a cappuccino in Little Italy, black patent leather S&M heels, two unfashionable tits stuffed into a pale green corset, and extremely fashionable black fake leather tights heaves her large self off a car top. She's holding an empty bottle.

Diego senses there's going to be trouble. He gets off his car top. Is walking slowly towards the girl.

The bottle keeps waving. Finally the girl finds some courage heaves the bottle at the skinny entrance artist.

The girl and the artist battle it out up the street. Some of the people who are sitting on cars separate them. We see the girl throw herself back on a car top. Her tits are bouncing so hard she must want our attention and she's getting insecure, maybe violent, cause she isn't getting enough. Better give us a better show. She sticks her middle finger into the air as far as she can. She writhes around on the top of the car. Her movements are so spasmodic she must be nuts.

A yellow taxi cab is slowly making its way to the club. On one side of this taxi cab's the club entrance. The other side is the girl writ(h)ing away on the black car. Three girls who are pretending to be transvestites are lifting themselves out of the cab elegantly around the big girl's body. The first body is encased into a translucent white girdle. A series of diagonal panels leads directly to her cunt. The other two dresses are tight and white. They are wriggling their way toward the club. The big girl, whom the taxi driver refused to let in his cab, wriggling because she's been rejected but not wriggling as much, is bumping into them. They're tottering away from her because she has syphilis.

Now the big girl is unsuccessfully trying to climb through a private white car's window now she's running hips hooking even faster into an alleyway taxi whose driver is locking his doors and windows against her. She's offering him a blow-job. Now an ugly boy with a huge safety pin stuck through his upper lip, walking up and down the street, is shooting at us with his watergun.

The dyke sitting next to me is saying earlier in the evening she pulled at this safety pin.

It's four o'clock A.M. It's still too hot. Wet heat's squeezing this city. The air's mist. The liquid's that seeping out of human flesh pores is gonna harden into a smooth shiny shell so we're going to become reptiles.

No one wants to move anymore. No one wants to be in a body. Physical possessions can go to hell even in this night.

Johnny like all other New York inhabitants doesn't want anything to do with sex. He hates sex because the air's hot, because feelings are dull, and because humans are repulsive.

Like all the other New Yorker's he's telling females he's strictly gay and males all faggots ought to burn in hell and they are. He's doing this because when he was sixteen years old his parents who wanted him to die stuck him in the Merchant Marines and all the marines cause this is what they do raped his ass off with many doses of coke.

Baudelaire doesn't go directly toward self-satisfaction cause of the following mechanism: X wants Y and, for whatever reasons reasons, thinks it shouldn't want Y. X thinks it is BAD because it wants Y. What X wants is Y and to be GOOD.

Baudelaire does the following to solve this dilemma: He understands that some agency (his parents, society, his mistress, etc.) is saying that wanting Y is BAD. This agency is authority is right. The authority will punish him because he's BAD. The authority will punish him as much as possible, punish me punish me, more than is necessary till it has to be obvious to everyone that the punishment is unjust. Punishers are unjust. All authority right now stinks to high hell. Therefore there is no GOOD and BAD. X cannot be BAD.

It's necessary to go to as many extremes as possible.

As soon as Johnny sees Janey he wants to have sex with her. Johnny takes out his cock and rubs it. He walks over to Janey, puts his arms around her shoulders so he's pinning her against a concrete wall.

Johnny says, "You're always talking about sex. Are you going to spread your legs for me like you spread your legs all the time for any guy you don't know?"

Janey replies, "I'm not fucking anymore cause sex is a prison. It's become a support of this post-capitalist system like art. Businessmen who want to make money have to turn up a product that people'll buy and want to keep buying. Since American consumers now own every object there is plus they don't have any money anyway cause they're being squeezed between inflation and depression, just like fucking, these businessmen have to discover products that obvious necessity sells. Sex is such a product. Just get rid of the puritanism sweetheart your parents spoonfed you in between materialism which the sexual revolution did thanks to free love and hippies sex is a terrific hook. Sexual desire is a naturally fluctuating phenomena. The sex product presents a naturally expanding market. Now capitalists are doing everything they can to bring world sexual desire to an unbearable edge.

"I don't want to be hurt again. Getting hurt or rejected is more dangerous than I know because now everytime I get sexually rejected I get dangerously physically sick. I don't want to hurt again. Everytime I hurt I feel so disgusted with myself — that by following some stupid body desire I didn't HAVE to follow, I killed the tender nerves of someone else. I retreat into myself. I again become frigid."

"I never have fun."

Johnny says, "You want to be as desperate as possible but you don't have to be desperate. You're going to be a success. Everybody knows you're going to be a success. Wouldn't you like to give up this artistic life which you know isn't rewarding cause artists now have to turn their work/selves into marketable objects/fluctuating images/fashion have to competitively knife each other in the back because we're not people, can't treat each other like people, no feelings, loneliness comes from the world of rationality, robots, every thing one as objects defined separate from each other? The whole impetus for art in the first place is gone bye-bye? You know you want to get away from this media world."

Janey replies, "I don't know what I want now. I know the New York City world is more complex and desirable even though everything you're saying's true. I don't know what my heart is cause I'm corrupted."

"Become pure again. Love. You have to will. You can do what you will. Then love'll enter your heart."

"I'm not capable of loving anyone. I'm a freak. Love's an obsession that only weird people have. I'm going to be a robot for the rest of my life. This is confusing to be a human being, but robotism is what's present."

42

"It's unnatural to be sexless. You eat alone and that's freaky."

"I am lonely out of my mind. I am miserable out of my mind. Open open what are you touching me. Touching me. Now I'm going into the state where desire comes out like a monster. Sex I love you. I'll do anything to touch you. I've got to fuck. Don't you understand don't you have needs as much as I have needs DON'T YOU HAVE TO GET LAID?"

—Janey, close that door. What's the matter with you? Why aren't you doing what I tell you?

—I'll do whatever you tell me, nana.

—That's right. Now go into that drawer and get that check-book for me. The Chase Manhattan one, not the other one. Give me both of them. I'll show you which one.

—I can find it, nana. No, it's not this one.

—Give me both of them. I'll do it.

—Here you are, nana. This is the one you want, isn't it?

—Now sit yourself down and write yourself out a check for $10,000. It doesn't matter which check you write it on.

—Ten thousand dollars! Are you sure about this, nana?

—Do what I tell you. Write yourself out a check for ten thousand dollars.

—Uh O.K. What's the date?

—It doesn't matter. Put any date you want. Now hand me my glasses. They're over there.

—I'm just going to clean them. They're dirty.

—You can clean them for me later. Give them to me.

—Are...you sure you want to do this?

—Now I'm going to tell you something, Janey. Invest this. Buy yourself 100 shares of AT&T. You can fritter it away if you want. Good riddance to you. If your mother had invested the 800 shares of IBM I gave her, she would have had a steady income and wouldn't have had to commit suicide. Well, she needed the money. If you invest in AT&T, you'll always have an income.

—I don't know what to say. I've never seen so much money before. I've never seen so much money before.

—You do what I tell you to. Buy AT&T.

—I'll put the money in a bank, nana, and as soon as it clears I'll buy AT&T.

At ten o'clock the next morning Nana is still asleep. A rich salesman who was spending his winter in New York had installed her in a huge apartment on Park Avenue for six months. The apartment's rooms are tremendous, too big for her tiny body, and are still partly unfurnished. Thick sick daybed spreads ivory-handled white feather fans hanging above contrast the black-and-red 'naturalistic' clown portraits in the 'study' that give an air of culture rather than of call-girl. A call-girl or mistress, as soon as her first man is gone, is no longer innocent. No one to help her, constantly harassed by rent and food bills, in need of elegant clothing and cosmetics to keep surviving, she has to use her sex to get money.

Nana's sleeping on her stomach, her bare arms hugging instead of a man a pillow into which she's buried a face soft with sleep. The bedroom and the small adjoining dressingroom are the only two properly furnished rooms. A ray of light filtered through the gray richly-laced curtain focuses a rosewood bedsteads covered by carved Chinese figures, the bedstead covered by white linen sheets; covered by a pale blue silk quilt; covered by a pale white silk quilt; Chinese pictures composed of five to seven layers of carved ivory, almost sculptures rather than pictures, surround these gleaming layers.

She feels around and, finding no one, calls her maid.

"Paul left ten minutes ago," the girl says as she walks into the room. "He didn't want to wake you. I asked him if he wanted coffee but he said he was in a rush. He'll see you his usual time tomorrow."

"Tomorrow tomorrow;" the prostitute can never get anything straight, "can he come tomorrow?"

"Wednesday's Paul's day. Today you see the furrier."

"I remember," she says, sitting up, "the old furrier told me he's coming Wednesday and I can't go against him. Paul'll have to come another day."

"You didn't tell me. If you don't tell me what's going on, I'm going to get things confused and your Johns'll be running into each other!"

Nana stretches her fatty arms over her head and yawns. Two bunches of short brown hairs are sticking out of her armpits. "I'll call Paul and tell him to come back tonight. No. I won't sleep with anyone tonight. Can I afford it? I'll tell Paul to come on Tuesdays after this and I'll have tonight to myself!" Her nightgown slips down her nipples surrounded by one long brown hair and the rest of her hair, loose and tousled, flows over her still-wet sheets.

Bet—I think feminism is the only thing that matters.

Janey (yawning)—I'm so tired all I can do is sleep all day (only she doesn't fall asleep cause she's suddenly attracted to Michael who's like every other guy she's attracted to married to a friend of hers.)

Bet—First of all feminism is only possible in a socialist state.

Janey—But Russia stinks as much as the United States these days. What has this got to do with your film?

Bet—Cause feminism depends on four factors: First of all, women have to have economic independence. If they don't have that they don't have anything. Second, free daycare centers. Abortions. (counting on her fingers) Fourth, decent housing.

Janey—I mean those are just material considerations. You're accepting the materialism this society teaches. I mean look I've had lots of abortions I can fuck anyone I want—well, I could—I'm still in prison. I'm not talking about myself.

Bet—Are you against abortions?

Janey—How could I be against abortions? I've had fucking five of them. I can't be against abortions. I just think all that stuff is back in the 1920's. It doesn't apply to this world. This world is different than all that socialism: those multi-national corporations control everything.

Louie—You just don't know how things are cause the feminist movement here is nothing compared to the feminist movements in Italy, England, and Australia. That's where women really stick together.

Janey—That's not true! Feminism here, sure it's not the old feminism the groups Gloria Steinem and Ti-Grace, but they were *so* straight. It's much better now: it's just underground it's not so public.

Louie—The only women in Abercrombie's and Fitch's films are those traditionally male defined types.

The women are always whores or bitches. They have no power.

Janey—Women are whores now. I think women every time they fuck no matter who they fuck should get paid. When they fuck their boyfriends their husbands. That's the way things are only the women don't get paid.

Louie—Look at Carter's films. There are no women's roles. The only two women in the film who aren't bit players are France who's a bitch and England who's a whore.

Janey—But that's how things were in Rome of that time.

Bet—But, Jane, we're saying things have to be different. Our friends can't keep upholding the sexist state of women in their work.

Janey—You know about Abercrombie and Fitch. I don't even bother saying anything to them. But Carter's film; you've got to look at why an artist does what he does. Otherwise you're not being fair. In ROME Carter's saying the decadent Roman society was like this one.

Louie—The one that a certain small group of artists in New York lives in.

Janey—Yeah .

Louie—He's saying the men we know treat women only as whores and bitches.

Janey—So what are you complaining about?

Bet—Before you were saying you have no one to talk to about your work. That's what I'm saying. We've got to tell Abercrombie and Fitch what they're doing. We've got to start portraying women as strong showing women as the power of this society.

Janey—But we're not.

Bet—But how else are we going to be? In Italy there was this women's art festival. A friend of ours who does performance dressed as a woman and did a performance. Then he revealed he was a man. The women in the festival beat him up and called the police.

Michael—The police?

Janey—Was he good?

Bet—He was the best performer there.

Louie—I think calling the police is weird. They should have just beaten him up.

Janey—I don't like the police.

I WANT ALL THE ABOVE TO BE THE SUN.

Janey dreams of cocks. Janey sees cocks instead of objects. Janey has to fuck.

This is the way Sex drives Janey crazy: Before Janey fucks, she keeps her wants in cells. As soon as Janey's fucking she wants to be adored as much as possible at the same time as, its other extreme, ignored as much as possible. More than this: Janey can no longer perceive herself wanting. Janey is Want.

It's worse than this: If Janey gets sexually rejected her body becomes sick. If she doesn't get who she wants she naturally revolts.

This is the nature of reality. No rationality possible. Only this is true. The world in which there is no feeling, the robot world, doesn't exist. This world is a very dangerous place to live in.

Old women just cause they're old and no man'll fuck them don't stop wanting sex.

The old actress isn't good anymore. But she keeps on acting even though she knows all the audiences mock her hideousness and lack of context cause she adores acting. Her legs are grotesque: FLABBY. Above, hidden within the folds of skin, there's an ugly cunt. Two long flaps of white thin spreckled by black hairs like a pig's cock flesh hang down to the knees. There's no feeling in them. Between these two flaps of skin the meat is red folds and drips a white slime that poisons whatever it touches. Just one drop burns a hole into anything. An odor of garbage infested by maggots floats out of this cunt. One wants to vomit. The meat is so red it looks like someone hacked a body to bits with a cleaver or like the bright red lines under the purple lines on the translucent skin of a woman's body found dead three days ago. This red leads to a hole, a hole of redness, round and round, black nausea. The old actress is black nausea because she reminds us of death. Yet she keeps plying her trade and that makes her trade weird. Glory be to those humans who are absolutely NOTHING for the opinions of other humans: they are the true owners of illusions, transformations, and themselves.

Old people are supposed to be smarter than young people.

Old people in this country the United States of America are treated like total shit. Since most people spend their lives mentally dwelling on the material, they have no mental freedom, when they grow old and their skin rots and their bodies turn to putrefying sand and they can't do physical exercise and they can't indulge in bodily pleasure and they're all ugly anyway; suddenly they got nothing. Having nothing, you think they could at least be shut up in opiated dens so maybe they have a chance to develop dreams or at least they could warn their kids to do something else besides being materialistic. But the way this country's set up, there's not even opiated homes to hide this feelinglessness: old people have to go either to children's or most often into rest homes where they're shunted into wheelchairs and made as fast as possible into zombies cause it's easier to handle a zombie, if you have to handle anything, than a human. So an old person has a big empty hollow space with nothing in it, just ugh, and that's life: nothing else is going to happen, there's just ugh stop.

ANYTHING THAT DESTROYS LIMITS

Afterwards Janey and Johnny went to an all-night movie. All during the first movie Janey's sort of leaning against Johnny cause she's unsure he's attracted to her and she doesn't want to embarrass him (her) in case he ain't. She kinda scrunches against him. One point Johnny is pressing his knee against her knee but she still ain't sure.

Some Like It Hot ends. All the rest of the painters are gonna leave the movie house cause they've seen *The Misfits*. Separately Janey and Johnny say they're going to stay. The painters are walking out. The movie theater is black.

Janey still doesn't know what Johnny's feelings are.

A third way through the second movie Johnny's hand grabs her knee. Her whole body becomes crazy. She puts her right hand into his hand but he doesn't want the hand.

Johnny's hand, rubbing her tan leg, is inching closer to her cunt. The hand is moving roughly, grabbing handfuls of flesh, the flesh and blood crawling. He's not responding to anything she's doing.

Finally she's tentatively touching his leg. His hand is pouncing on her right hand setting it an inch below his cock. Her body's becoming even crazier and she's more content.

His other hand is inching slower toward her open slimy hole. Cause the theater is small, not very dark, and the seats aren't too steep, everyone sitting around them is watching exactly what

48

they're doing: Her black dress is shoved up around her young thighs. His hand is almost curving around her darkpantied cunt. Her and his legs are intertwined. Despite fear she's sure to be arrested just like in a porn book because fear she's wanting him to stick his cock up her right now.

His hand is roughly travelling around her cunt, never touching nothing, smaller and smaller circles.

Morning. The movie house lights go on. Johnny looks at Janey like she's a business acquaintance. From now on everything Janey does is for the purpose of getting Johnny's dick into her.

Johnny, "Let's get out of here."

New York City at six in the morning is beautiful. Empty streets except for a few bums. No garbage. A slight shudder of air down the long long streets. Pale gray prevails. Janey's going to kill Johnny if he doesn't give her his cock instantaneously. She's thinking ways to get him to give her his cock. Her body becomes even crazier. Her body takes over. Turn on him.

Throw arms around his neck. Back him against car. Shove clothed cunt against clothed cock. Lick ear because that's what there is.

Lick your ear.

Lick your ear.

Well?

I don't know.

What don't you know? You don't know if you want to?

Turn on him. Throw arms around his neck. Back him against car. Shove clothed cunt against clothed cock. Lick ear because that's what there is.

Obviously I want to.

I don't care what you do. You can come home with me; you can take a rain check; you cannot take a rain check.

I have to see my lawyer tomorrow. Then I have lunch with Ray.

Turn on him. Throw arms around his neck. Back him against car. Shove clothed cunt against clothed cock. Lick ear because that's what there is.

You're not helping me much.

You're not helping me much.

Through this morning they walk to her apartment. Johnny and Janey don't touch. Johnny and Janey don't talk to each other.

Johnny is saying that Janey's going to invite him up for a few minutes.

Janey is pouring Johnny a glass of Scotch. Janey is sitting in her bedroom on her bed. Johnny is untying the string holding up her black sheath. Johnny's saliva-wettened fingers are pinching her nipple. Johnny is lifting her body over his prostrate body. Johnny's making her cunt rub very roughly through the clothes against his huge cock. Johnny's taking her off him and lifting her dress over her body. Janey's saying, "Your cock is huge." Janey's placing her lips around Johnny's huge cock. Janey's easing her black underpants over her feet.

Johnny's moaning like he's about to come. Janey's lips are letting go his cock. Johnny's lifting Janey's body over his body so the top of his cock is just touching her lips. His hands on her thighs are pulling her down fast and hard. His cock is so huge it is entering her cunt painfully. His body is immediately moving quickly violently shudders. The cock is entering the bottom of Janey's cunt. Janey is coming. Johnny's hands are not holding Janey's thighs firmly enough and Johnny's moving too quickly to keep Janey coming. Johnny is building up to coming.

That's all right yes I that's all right. I'm coming again smooth of you oh oh smooth, goes on and on, am I coming am I not coming.

Janey's rolling off of Johnny. Johnny's pulling the black pants he's still wearing over his thighs because he has to go home. Janey's telling him she has to sleep alone even though she isn't knowing what she's feeling. At the door to Janey's apartment Johnny's telling Janey he's going to call her. Johnny walks out the door and doesn't see Janey again.

LUST

A SAILOR'S SLIGHT IDENTITY

Because he's alone, a sailor's always telling himself who he is:

Due to the increasing conservatism of this government, the cops're enforcing more and tighter restrictions on every area of the private sector. Even the hippies and punks're no longer rioting. Capture by the German cops means torture or, at best, slavery. Thus, in Berlin, I was an insect I am going to describe the life of vermin.

Burroughs said that writers are insects. Without lives. Like sailors. A writer's one type of sailor, a person without human relationships.

Cold winds sweep over our dead rats; a dead terrorist's heart sits on dogshit. Mutilated police calls, advertising leaflets spell SOS. I liked watching and reading about two men stroking each other's penises. When I reached Berlin, one morning when the street beyond my window was almost the color of diarrheic dog turd from the rain, I saw two men who were obviously a couple. One told the other, a small bastardy-looking shit, "I'll get the groceries."

I didn't leave: I had nothing better to do than wait for someone whom I didn't know to return. About two hours later, he returned with a small bag. I wanted to follow him back to his room; I didn't; I knew that following him would be useless.

Through condoms and orange peels, mosaics of newspapers floating in small pools of water and piss, down into the ooze with gangsters in concrete and pistols pounded flat to avoid ballistic detection.

I like looking at men who've got muscles. Short bodies. These men look like bastards. They're the ones who act, who can act.

They give their energy. When I look at one, I have him and I lean my head right back into his chest. Between his large hand and his stomach, there, it's warm. There I'm safe. Since he makes

51

me safe, I'll do anything for him. I know this sexuality, who I am, is nothing to be proud of: I am almost nothing. But I can't hate myself.

The muscular man's erection was hardening. The two men kept their mouths soldered together with tongues either crushed or sharp tips in contact. A knife cannot cut through another knife. Neither dared to place his tongue on the other's cheek for a kiss is a sign of vulnerability. By mistake a pair of eyes now and then caught the other pair of eyes. Then they hid. Snakes. Tongues were as hard as metal. The pricks are harder than tongues.

If I'm to go on living, I have to accept my sexuality.

I never knew my dad. He had left my mother for good six months before I was born. He had never wanted to meet me.

Though very little of my time is devoted to fucking, often none for months, I think constantly about sex and sexuality. It was about 4: 20 A M. in a Communist Chinese hotel in Germany. Two narrow and separated beds were nailed to the floor. There was a thin grey carpet. There were two small towels. There was a wardrobe. There was a table. There were four upright chairs. There was a telephone. I had left my ship about two days ago.

A man, whom I knew slightly, a criminal type, phoned. He told me that I was lonely and he'd be good for me. I wanted to ask him questions which I was too shy to ask a stranger—

(1) Do you want to fuck me in the ass?

(2) Do you want to fuck me in the ass more than once?

Three weeks later I met this man in another town in Germany. His body was short. His muscles slightly inclined to fat. After two hours we kissed. I continued to kiss him harder faster, with rising and more cunningly, here there, quick little pecks as my tough, very wide lips moved nearer his left ear. Every animal finds a home or dies. Finally I placed my tongue in an ear which was dirty.

The tongue moved around the thick ear. I placed my cheek against his teeth because I wanted him to bite me hard. Like big warm animals hug, he held me in arms as wide as my torso.

He was a sailor.

I tried to grab his huge head and pull it down as if I were wrestling. At the same time the rest of me was pressing into him, especially his lower body, and twining my legs around his so that our genitals could meet and rub through the wool.

In this warmth which we had created we remained together. I kept kissing and rubbing the bullet head, then kissing his male skin everywhere. Rubbing the skin or mind into need.

Want rose up, the sailor.

At last I found myself about to ejaculate. I wanted to prolong this need, whose appearance was physical, into total desperation, into the most desperate need which is possible, that is, not possible. But it was impossible to remain living in the impossible.

No longer could I distinguish between lust and love. I wanted to smear KY over his, Mick's, cock. Rusty barges, red brick building, graffiti of dead anarchists on the wall, only because he was going to hurt me, I fantasized the possibility that he would hurt me. Why do I get off on being rejected? I don't care. Cut off a leg and another limb grows stronger. Our generation came out of mutilation. We wear our mutilations as badges; wearing badges is the only possibility we have for human love. I fantasized that his penis was not very long and was thick. A penis that looked like a boxer, if a boxer could look like a penis.

When I had first noticed him in Hamburg, I had been sitting next to him. I remember that I looked down and saw a large lump in old grey pants. The thighs were heavy and spread apart, as if the hill would rise up in between....At the same time as I saw this, I noticed I was staring at the lump. I wouldn't have been conscious of my fascination if I had thought that there were any sexual attraction between us.

At last I found myself about to ejaculate. I let the hand that was perching on Mick's shoulder slide down his back till it reached the buttocks. The buttocks were moving. I put my hand around this quivering, still clothed flesh and took possession of it. I slipped my hand up, and under the trouser belt and the white undershirt in front. I touched the penis. I forced myself to do what I wanted to do.

I was in that being or state where only sex matters.

My other hand took hold of one of his thick hands and forced it to touch my penis. Dolphins leapt about the prow and flying fish scattered before us almost in golden showers. Mick stroked the naked penis under the wool trousers, then on his own accord unbuttoned my flap. Dead leaves falling, jagged slashes of blue sky where the boards curled as if from fire apart. Mick squeezed my penis so hard that I whispered for a suck. Mick bent down only the upper part of his body and parted his lips. Violet twilight yellow-gray around the edges, color of human brains. While he was kneeling in front of me, Mick was sucking my cock so red it was obscene.

Whereas the slums in Hamburg are the slums of its sailors, Berlin is a big slum. For everyone. Except the tourist section

53

which is fake shit for the foreigners. Just as the USA is fake shit because of a few people's manipulations. But playgrounds die. The English Labour Party holds hands and sings "Auld Lang Syne."

The Barrio Chino, a section in Berlin only known to Berlin's dedicated alcoholics and speed shooters, is a geographical foulness inhabited, not by Spanish sailors nor by the American Merchant Marine, nor by the Turks, but by those who have been separate so long from their birthplaces or anything resembling home, they are nationless. As long as they are alive, lost. The Barrio Chino is a place for drifters. Loneliness rather than sex has become the last vestige of capitalism. Loneliness is both a disease and a cause of personal strength.

These sadistic and masochistic drifters resemble the criminals who lived in the American and German urban conglomerates prior to the emergence of crime as international monopoly before human relationships degenerated into piss. Before the filth and disorder of the Barrio Chino. Long ropes hang between sailors legs.

Sardine can cut open with scissors...shoehorn has been used as spoon...dirty sock in a plate of moldy beans...toothpaste smear on washstand glass...cigarette butt ground out in cold scrambled eggs...the children of the Barrio Chino.

An apartment at no. 10-11 Bayermalle on Holy Sunday, November 10, 1974, when all the virgins were singing loneliness. Someone rang its doorbell. Through the intercom, the doorbell ringer said he was delivering flowers. (The owner of this flat, Günter von Drenkmann, President of the Superior Court of Justice and Berlin's senior judge, was celebrating his 64th birthday.) When the door was opened, one of the youths outside pushed the door wide open. Another kid shot at Drenkmann three times and hit him twice.

Then all of these kids escaped in one Peugeot and one Mercedes. They obviously had stolen the cars. The old judge died.

The first penis I saw in Berlin was so beautiful I died. Before that I had thought that I was living in boredom. With this I found a community. Penises were lice. Sometimes they were crabs through whom I could see. Water seeped through the rotting walls upward into more rotting materials. The flesh melted into ooze. I wanted to tear down these walls, the ooze, to enter fully into Mick. To mingle in the way that no flesh can mingle. Mick was my mirror, my wall. I knew for a moment I was his. But the

54

owners of the walls, the landlords, wouldn't let us tear them down. Owners hate sailors. Even owners who believe in liberalism, for democracy's other side is crime.

Every now and then, for instance when the President of the United States came to town, the Barrio Chino held a riot. Hatred made us erect.

Mick and I lived together for six months. He wasn't my greatest fuck. But I didn't care because he was the scum I wanted. I had no family and he wasn't going to be one, but for six months I got fucked. We parted for good without a reason.

Two nights after we had parted, in a bar whose walls and ceiling were aluminum, I picked up another sailor. As the sailor was sliding a hand up to my testicles from the back, I strangled him in the bar's back room. No one in the bar cared about my strangulation. Islands isolated in madness. I watched his life ebbing (refuse) under the pressure of my clenched, tightened fingers (refusés), watched the sailor die with mouth agape (refused) tongue out (speechless), watched the crisis of my solitary pleasures (refusal). City of flesh shrivelled in aluminum bars, yellow couches, tables covered in speed dust. I killed him because I needed to be rejected by you who are alive. Only then would I find a community of those who are like me.

By murdering I raise myself out of the death in which I'm living. When I murdered the sailor, a miraculous wave broke into the silence of my ears (no one to whom to talk), the silence of my mouth (no one to whom to talk): the world started humming.

At this point I had no friends. The only thing there is to talk about now is isolation. Though my murdering had come from isolation—isolation is always insupportable—my murdering also announced my isolation to the world and so provided the first step toward destroying isolation. Afterwards I could only turn to other murderers. To those who realized they were sick. We are the failures on, not the governors of, this earth. Consciousness of our failure allowed us to be friends. The diseased fear only poverty. For all else is theirs and not to be feared: isolation, the ravages of sexual needs, ravaging sexual need, misunderstanding, autism, visual and audial hallucination, paranoia

This night which has lasted for a long time I want to say that I cannot stand isolation anymore. The only way I see out of isolation is murder. Which makes isolation. This, in a sense, is my ode to the Baader-Meinhof, a group of kids who didn't fully consider the consequences of going against the law of the land, of ownership, became mad. This endless night.

Here I am alone.

In Berlin, something beside isolation happened. In the middle of a night I drove around in a car with two other people with a cassette blaring out Marc Almond and Neubauten. In that country where the bourgeoisie are so stolid, they are immovable fairytales: isolated from the world and from myself, doubly isolated, I found friends.

The next day the cops tried to find the sailor's, Joachim's, murderer. I didn't feel guilty because I had murdered a Jew. The cops decided that a black man, another sailor, whose name was the name of a pariah, had murdered my sailor.

Perhaps it was out of guilt that the court sentenced Jonah to an early execution. Jonah was executed.

Now, I wanted to forget. Not my murder, but the world that had wrongly condemned Jonah, the world that condemned my murder, the world that, or rather who, caused isolation. I wanted to disappear. I wanted to disappear from this world into the night. I knew that it was impossible to kill myself.

Weil er mein Freund ist, liebt er mich. The cops weren't going to learn that I had actually murdered the sailor because the cops were snouts. The next man I fucked was a cop. I insisted that what I wanted most was that he pierce my throat as far as possible and fill it with slime.

I won't kiss but I get off on sucking the prick of a man whom I detest. Because I'm penetrating myself. When I was sucking the dick's prick, I was able to go beyond myself. At the same time, I was frightened: I would lose control and bite the cock too hard, which wouldn't be a bad thing, but, on the other hand, cops are human. Sucking this hot cock made my own despair and nothingness or my death apparent to me.

How black Berlin.

While I was thinking this in the act of sucking him off, the cop moaned, "I'm a cop. I'm a cop and I'm a creep. Cause I make it with guys. *Weil er mein Freund ist, liebt er mich.* I'm homosexual. I make it with every punk I can get. Then I shove the kid into jail so that I can have him whenever I want. I put the kid in jail cause that's what I like. I like putting the kid into jail after making him do what both of us want. My hands control his mouth."

The more this cop confessed through his muttering, confessed to a sailor he didn't know, and it didn't matter in the slime of Berlin, what slime he was, the more he became a hero to me. After only a little while more I would do anything for this big man. I loved being like this. It was like being someone else. Or being someone. In an unknown place of wonder, I would grovel at the cop's feet and, then, like a puppy, try to nip the cop's ankles. Big cops wear boots because they ride BMWs. When his sperm was visible and dead, the cop and I had nothing to say to each other.

Nothing new was happening in the city. It was time to leave. It's not that the Nazis had ruined a world. The Nazis had changed nothing. Dead cops don't fuck; death breeds only death. My nostrils were stinking of the smegma in my belly and the smegma on the streets so it was time to leave.

I went back to my ship where I carried out my duties impeccably. For there's no reason not to do exactly what I'm told to do even by scum.

Back in Berlin the cop rose in his work He became a lieutenant. Seeing that his career was beginning, finally sure of himself to be master of his domain. decay: he began to do as he pleased.

Bits of what I wrote at sea:

> I find myself alone. I'm safe because the ocean surrounds me like when I was a child. I no longer have to be an animal crazy in its foraging for food. Society appears to be largely composed of extremists and habitual criminals not normal human animals subjects or citizens of respectable states. But I have no more community here cause sailors aren't usually murderers: sailors are nothing. I have had to decide, because I'm on the edge of suicide, that loneliness, like poverty, is a test. I no longer understand anything that is happening to me.

I wrote this about my murder:

> When that grief that is beyond tears, that tears the griever apart, that grief over a human death, fades: emptiness remains. The shock that a demi-god, one to whom one has given suck, can die becomes only the shock of death: the dead person *cannot* be dead. Death, above all, is impossible. That is: unthinkable.
>
> Besides shock all the other to-do surrounding murder or political assassination is a hypocritical way of pretending that the demi-god or human cannot be replaced in our society *which is actually a world of*

interchangeable puppets. Of pretending that there are still human individuals, that these individuals still make history, when in fact all that we individuals—sailors—can now do is wish to act, exert ineffective wills, talk endlessly about human morality (do animals have morality?), when in fact the autonomous mechanisms of social repression have been and are being reproduced in every individual.

A world of interchangeable puppets...unless you starve...the autonomous mechanisms of social repression...unless you starve...inevitably reproduced in every individual...

...an eroticized state...

In this society of total, not so much conformity, but homogenization, pasteurization beyond what the fifties' sociologists envisaged, we're making signs to each other that we're unlike by displaying disease or murdering. It's hard to be friends. Though we both know we're evil, I wonder whether or not we'll be friends. I make mistakes, often out of impatience, by imagining that there's camaraderie when there's not

I wrote this about romanticism which comes after murder:

I first came to Berlin when I was twenty. I found whatever I was looking for there, though I said I couldn't name it. I first came to Berlin when I was twenty for some reason which I didn't know. Before I was in Berlin, I stole motorcycles and bashed them up in Munich. They didn't like me there because I'm very quiet. Too quiet. Until they show they hate me and then my back's against the wall and then I go mad. I become violent. I hate most of all being shut up or bored. Say that I hate everyone and every social thing. Me: I believe in romanticism. Romanticism *is* the world. Why? Because there's got to be something. There has to be something for we who are and know that we're homeless.

When I returned, not to Berlin, but to Hamburg in the midst of the fog of the beginning of winter, to the road that runs right above its river and docks, a castle which never existed and a fountain which is really a sewer, a gust of wind far sweeter and more fragrant than any red rose carried the smell of shit and floating soil like a tongue into my nostril.

It was late at night. As yet there were no dreams. I wondered when dreams would come to me, when the real dreams would come, dreams of something besides sailors. I wondered where they were. Like a man who wants to sleep and can't, so tries without success to know sleep. Wondered when the muscles of my face would be released, when my eyelids would blink more slowly, when the last light would die. When soft, gentle, and not just from weariness, you would lay on your back. Still in your sailor's uniform.

Tender and gentle, you then run your hands between my buttocks as if you're loving me there. Out of modesty, a form of fear perhaps, frightened that your prick is soiled by my asshole shit, I clean it with my free hand. My other hand, already seeking your hair in order to touch it, meets the face and strokes the cheek instead.

No love can be expressed between us. Love doesn't exist between us. We know only our varied musculature which has developed out of pain. You say that only fiction or language could inform us that we love each other. Perhaps this is true. But it's for other reasons that we understand what we mean when we speak together, our grunts, our solipsisms. Without the musculature which comes from pain no one is understood. With both hands clinging, one to an ear, the other to your hair, I wrench your head away from my axis which is getting harder.

Whenever you have sex with someone, you partially become each other.

After this sailor had finished cocksucking, I strangled him. Abandoned by parents, by friends, by America, by the pricks I had sucked, I knew that above all I hated, not death, but giving up to death.

DEAD PEOPLE DON'T FUCK

El marinero degollado
Cantaba el oso de agua que lo había de estrechar.

There were three poets. The three poets were ugly old men. They had once been hippies, but they were no longer hippies. They thought that without their visions, this city would dissolve. Without their dreams, the city would dissolve. This city is dissolving anyway. Being into love, the poets had nothing to celebrate

They were just like snakes who, not having anything to eat, eat their own tails. When snakes eat themselves out, they think

59

they are the only thing there is. More and more of the people are hungry.

There was a falling-down church. The church was a hideout for Puerto Rican terrorists. A young woman leapt up from one of the church pews, there weren't many of them, as if her ass was full of tracks, but it was just tacky. She was lean and brown; her gown was pink; she began to slink just like a slinky fat rat forwards and back:

I'm gwine down to de river
Set me down on de ground
If the blues overtake me,
Gon' jump overboard and drown.

It was one of the weekly readings in the Puerto Rican terrorist church.

Not this.

The church was called "St. Marks-in-the-Bowery." In an urban environment, a "bowery" is a bum refuge. Bums of all kinds including sexual genders lived on its doorsteps and everywhere inside and outside this church. The Puerto Ricans lived underneath the graves. Every now and then a gang of children dug up a grave. Since the bums lived everywhere in the city, they were taking over the city just like the cockroaches had already taken the walls.

One of the three old men was just about to begin to read his poetry. In his mind, or in the depths of his soul, what he was about to begin to read was jazz. Because he liked garbage, he wrote poetry by picking phrases out of the cultural garbage cans—newspapers, sex mags, tv coverage, great poems, everything else—and stringing these phrasings together according to inaudible musical rhythms. He would have been reading to a sax, but the saxophonist had died ten years before. The poet didn't notice much outside him and he didn't have opinions.

Not this.

The church's audience were friends (other old poets), students, and bums. The students weren't yuppies, but revolutionary radicals and non-revolutionary radicals who aspired to the radicalness of bums. A few of the latter radicals had come in order to burn the church down. The bums had come in to escape the cold. The church wasn't heated. No one gave a damn about the reading.

Just as the old poet was about to read, a bum said, "Ah. Ah

60

feels like cutting me some white motherraper's throat." For a moment, someone was silent.

"We'll burn down the church," one student whispered to another.

Not this.

"Kill all the poets cause they're dead," another student who wasn't a poet said in a slightly louder voice.

"I'll say! Cause religion sucks!"

"No, it doesn't cause poets should be crucified."

Dick, the old poet who was about to read, ignored these cat-calls, knowing he was above them, being a poet, mainly cause he was frightened. So he stammered out, "Pope...Pope Pius the Sixth...Pope Pope." Maybe he thought that he was more famous than he was.

Not this.

Then remembering, then becoming lost in the wonder of his imagination, he started reading:

give us all honest work
to fuck every girl here
Annie Joanne Suzie Bern
I suppose
the main thrust is
knowledge
Cordelia sucked off Lear
daddy came too late
death, you come
no system
above meaningless tragedy
any other organ

Just as a revolutionary student pulled out a Magnum in order to halt the advance of immoral apolitical destructive artistic non-sense, one of the other old men, since he didn't notice the gun, limped toward the podium in order to extricate his friend from the masses' growing hostility. Tall and thin, this poet, pasty-faced, three hairs away from bald, for years his mouth frozen by speed into a smile, signalled to his friend to shut up.

At the same time, a bum walked into the church.

Not this.

There were many bums in the church. That's how society is. This bum appeared visible because his right hand was holding his left hand and his left hand wasn't holding anything like an

61

arm. He wasn't a writer. His left foot stood opposite to the way it should have stood. He walked, as much as he was able, to the backmost pew and perched up there like a great huge vulture.

Now Dick began to read a love poem to his wife:

> There is no way
> to find me
> while I find many
> cunts, my Muse ...

The bum took out his tiny cock and began to rub its head as if it was a dog. Finally, the students noticed that something was happening.

The bum, paying attention to the attention he and his dog were drawing, cried out to Dick, "Give to the poor."

Dick was now invoking Venus for some reason or other, probably a poetic one.

Not this.

"Shit and fuck," one of the non-revolutionary students said to another, "that's the bum who thinks he's a cop. He's always trying to arrest another bum. Here ya' go," the student threw a dead animal heart into the cop's lap.

"Come to me, my lady," said Dick

"Give to the poor," murmured the cop as the dead heart hit his other cheek

At this signal for war, over a hundred bums, who had forgotten to pay attention to the first signal, swarmed into the church in order to further their plan of taking over the city. Churches are major property owners. Thinking that all these new people were here to hear his poetry, Dick exclaimed:

> you took my love so tenderly
> with lips.

The bum in the back proceeded to show how.

Not this.

Mayor Koch, various church officials, and other government and real-estate agents were walking through this church in order to get rid of poverty and clean up the filth who were left. One of the real-estate men, casually dressed in bluejeans, said, "Poetry is shit."

The crowd agreed with him.

"Shit," yelled the members of the religious congregation.

"Shit."

"Shit."

Not this.

"Let's elect our own mayor," a bum said. Poverty changes the mind.

Cut to the quick and deeply hurt, Mayor Koch and his cohorts, criminal and otherwise, scrambled through walls of bums and ran away from the church's graves.

Now came the election of their Mayor of New York. In order to maintain democratic procedure, the students smashed one of the stained glass panels over the altar. The bums watched other people work. Whoever desired to be mayor would stick his or her face through the broken glass. The populace could choose the image they wanted to rule them.

Not this.

The poor want their own mirror. The world was created in the image of God.

Dick was reading his poetry.

"I'm just trying to sell coca-cola," one of the bums explained. "I'm not doing anything illegal." This bum was a big bum who once had had some muscle. Now his clothes didn't do much to hide his lack of muscles. "I dropped into this church just so I's could patronize my customers."

"You're under arrest." The bum who thought he was a cop.

"No, I ain't, cause I ain't done nothin' wrong."

Not this.

"He doesn't want to arrest you, " another bum explained to the coca-cola dealer. "He just wants some coke to put between his girlfriend's legs."

The bum who thought he was a pig flicked open a switch and slashed the upper half of the coke dealer's arm.

The poets except for Dick left the church because they didn't want to vote.

Not this.

"Coke's an evil drink," one explained. "It destroys the human mind."

The first candidate for mayoralty was sticking his head through the broken glass. He was a man. The upper half of the face looked like a fox's immediately after a wolf's eaten it. The whites of his eyes were red. The lower half was all mouth. Lips composed of red mucus membrane covered by white pustules stretched over the whole.

Not this.

Even though this one looked like a poet, the mass didn't want him. He didn't look like he had cancer.

There was some blood on the floor.

The next contestant was old enough to be a politician, so he had no sexual gender much less sex and, besides that, he, or it was dead. Just as if it had cancer. Cancer-Nose. Some uneducated bum yelled things at this face in the hope that it would die.

Not this.

"Coffin-fucker!"

"Infidel!"

Many Muslims live in New York City.

The next image was that of an English rose. The image of an English rose is more beautiful, fragile, than that of a poet, but the poet's is more metaphysical. John Donne, the poet, wrote:

> Since so, my minde
> Shall not desire what no man else can finde,
>   I'll no more dote and runne
> To pursue things which had indammag'd me.

Moreover, this face was deader than the dead man's face, for this face contained a dead soul. Hippies fuck a lot. The populace wasn't bothered to vote anymore.

"She doesn't have any tits!"

Not this.

Dick, the only poet left, was so upset by the anti-feminism that he had decided to show that poetry is more powerful than politics.

cunt ass-fucking cuntface cunthead cunt-hair smidgen tad cunt-lapper muff-diver cunt-lapping cunt meat cunt-struck diddle finger-fuck quiff roundheel quim pussy pussy-whipped asstail eatin' stuffwood pussy pussy butterfly pussy posse twat box clit clit-licker button puta dick clipped dick does a wooden horse have a hickory dick donkey dick limp-dick step on it dick-brained dick head dickey-licker screw goat fuck put the screws to someone throw a fuck into someone rag curse chew the fat on the rag take the rag off the bush randy rim ream cocksucker twink skosh smegma suck suck ass cocksucker suck face suck off blow scum scumbag rubber scumsucker scupper sucker suck-and-swallow piss eyes like pissholes in the snow full of piss and vinegar

64

not to have a pot to piss in panther piss a piss hard-on
piss-hole bandit piss bones piss pins and needles piss-
proud pisser tickle the shit out of someone shit crap poo
does a bear shit in the woods doodle-shit eat shit full of
shit have shit for brains holy shit horse shit shit-hole
shit-hunter shit-locker shittle-cum-shaw like pigs in
clover like shit through a tin horn like ten pounds of shit
in a five pound bag piece of shit pile of shit scare the
shit out of someone skin rubber condom get under
someone's skin press the flesh

Though he hated feelings and cunts, he continued this poem:

O muse! Female muse!
Our children no longer see
no longer care
for dreams.
Syphilis lies on their face;
herpes on our testicles.
My heart has closed up
scared to exist.

Doe- or black-eyed pre-pubescent whores stood on the streetcorner outside this church, swapped obscenities with the twitch-
ing junkies. The methadone center was four blocks away. Gangs
of slightly older muggers crouched in the narrow alleyways
between the church and the slim buildings, not yet architecturally
gentrified, but soaring up in rent every month. Pigeons died. The
teenagers were waiting to rob someone, but there was no one to
rob except each other and that wasn't much fun. In the gutters,
young kids played "Junkie" and "Whore". Uncollected torn
garbage cans, rotting vegetables, broken glass, used condoms,
crushed beer and coke cans, dog and human piss and shit against
the bottoms of the buildings. Big-tit moms, images of the Holy
Virgin Mary, standing at the edges of the tenements, talked about
God, unemployed, men, hunger, disease, religion, and Jews.
    Not this.
    "I ain't God," a man said as he showed his face through the
broken glass inside the church.
    "He ain't got no tits!"
    Orange hair would have sprouted out of this man's mon-
goloid head if he had any hair. Instead, he had a few brains. A
sole strand of gray spittle fell below his chin. Just like Ronald

Reagan's hair if Ronald Reagan had any real hair. Or Nancy's if she had real hair on her cunt. His face was actually ugly because it was the color of a dead person's who's been hibernating in the East River for ten days. They say that alligators crawl out of the sewers into that river and have to have their stomachs pumped. The East River's sister is the Thames and the dead are dead. Dead people don't fuck. Just like my mom when she was alive. Vomit would have been prettier than the collection of characteristics on this face. Only prettiness is no criterion for high literary quality. His was the face of a literary patriarch, for his wrinkles resembled a compilation of Mr Reagan's, Margaret Thatcher's, and the asshole of a purple-assed baboon who's just been diarrheic. Man descended from the monkey.

Not this.

The populace of bums and students liked this one so they clapped for a long time and hard for him. In this manner, they elected their own Mayor. As soon as they had voted him in, they forgot about him which shows bums are dumb.

The living gargoyle didn't reply to any of this because he couldn't reply because he didn't have a tongue.

"Steal away to Jesus," one bum replied for him, "steal away to Jesus," as his meaty black bones stole a wallet away and then skipped the light fantastic on one of his other bones.

Not this.

Since there was a certain lack of money among all but the rich in New York City, some of the bums were female. One of the females, while she was crying, looked at a bum and said, "I've got to say how much I want someone to care for me and I thought it was you. But it wasn't. It isn't." Crying.

"Because what I want is not what you want."

She raised her bald head up. "If a person's ugly, not evil or malicious, lust ugly, everyone rejects that person. Countries ban that person. West Germany, a country in which men drink piss at parties, bans that person. That person now cannot stop being ugly and so is unrelievably ugly.

"No one's ugly to themselves. Cause you don't see yourself. As far as seeing yourself goes: you're only seen. So an ugly person is ugly everywhere at all times. That's what ugliness's about."

Not this.

It seemed to the Mayor of New York that he was so ugly, he could not speak. So he looked for a shiv.

When a white student saw the black man looking for a shiv, he shot the ugly man. The ugly man's face contorted as he flopped on it into the lap of a bag-lady. His ugly face fell on her hand and bit it.

"Lesbian!" the bag-lady yelled, jumped up, and stamped on her mayor. "Perverts ought to be shot."

Not this.

Two more bums leaned down and turned the just-living gargoyle over on to his back; one tied one of his old Eton ties around the bleeding hand. The other stuck one of the pew legs in to tighten the tourniquet. The bum's other arm had been shot off.

The bum who had inserted the pew leg carefully into the hole looked up and found the bag-lady's pussy. 'You're a bum."

"No, she's not," the other bum told him. "She's a he."

Not this.

At this revelation of the transvestism lying rank in their ranks, the coca-cola dealer stood up, though his body was tottering, and proclaimed, "Jes' sit down, folks. All of you sit down. The coke'll be here sooner than a dead man can hear a pin drop. So everyone go back to his seat and pay up. We've called the fuzz so the coke'll be protected."

Not this.

And the sailor moved out to sea.

TOO NAKED

Dead time. A few not only leafless, but almost branchless trees stand in front of water which might be stone. Three large swans step out of the stone, shake themselves off, raise themselves up, living malignant monsters, as beautiful as the dying trees. They're looking for food which doesn't exist. The soil in front of them has been shoved and grooved into lumps by the feet of humans who no longer exist.

The sailor, Xovirax, speaks:

the judgement of Paris

I didn't wait for work to come. I got the first plane out of New York. On board I sat next to a boxer. He was slight for a boxer and had blond hair. He came back with me for a drink to the flat in London which another sailor had lent me. I thought how glad I was to be out of New York. He took off my clothes and didn't take his off. He told me to speak to him without asking him questions and he didn't reply in any way to anything that I said. I was unable to speak in such circumstances though I don't understand why. Then he told me to jerk myself off while he watched me and didn't watch me, without caring. He put an ungreased hand into my asshole and lifted me above his head. Every one-night-stand or man in a one-night-stand is like every other one-night-stand or man in a one-night-stand because the sex in a one-night-stand is without time and only time allows value.

For years I've been denying my own sexuality. I've been looking for what or whom I can't find.

What I want is what the boxer gave me. I didn't know how to reconcile this (something) with the fact of a one-night-stand (nothing).

I who have murdered.

"Tonight," the boxer said, "you're going to be dead. Tomorrow I'll be the one who's dead." Picking up my head, he added, "sailors who have short hair want to be hit."

after you cut off all my hair the rest of the upper part of my body you didn't touch also the lower part except to shove your fingers into my asshole I didn't know how many you got in there enough to carry me around by my asshole I guess you're a Grecian boxer though being a sailor I'm not well-educated though I've read a lot loneliness on the sea etc: you lifted me up by my asshole and carried me into a dark room. "I'm going to fetch another prisoner who's in the chicken coop in back I hope he won't put up too much of a fight he must trust me because I'm his policeman." you left me alone in the room.

I obediently lay there and waited for you to return or not to return.

a memory came to me I'm a kid I'm squiggled up against the doorway to my fathers and mother's bedroom I hear them talking about me SHE says, "Xovirax's so bad, he can't change." The WIMP agreed with her I was bad.

Then I heard you saying, "Let the accused rise have you anything to say in your own behalf?"

"It doesn't matter what I say," I said to you, "cause you aren't listening. You love me and you don't care about me."

"We'll chose the tortures," lots of voices said, "but first we have to invent the crimes. He's so small he's so pitiful even disgusting this sailor. He's not just anything. You can say and do anything to him. He's so contemptible, he wouldn't react. He isn't worth having a crime."

"He isn't worth punishing."

"No!" I cried cause absence's the worst punishment of all. But since you weren't in the room to hear me, it didn't matter what I said.

The boxer came back into the room. "OK You pinched my jackknife."

"I didn't pinch your jackknife."

"how come I found it under your pillow."

"you did not you're a liar."

the boxer pinched me, "besides that you stole my Good Humor bar and ate it."

I couldn't bear this torture so I passed out. While I was passed out, he stuck his cock up my asshole and I came.

when you're not here I can't decide whether you're not here because you don't care about me or you're not here because you like to hurt me. there're people in this world who like to hurt other people. they're the only people who can touch me.

it's either a fact or a common belief that every mother loves her child. when I was a child, I couldn't tell whether or not my mother loved me. she hated me, but because she was my mother, I couldn't believe that she hated me. ambiguity is more painful to me than hatred.

Night after night I lay alone in that room. The boxer didn't return. I decided that he didn't care about me. I decided that he was breaking me so that life could come out and be joyful. I decided that he didn't care what he was doing to me. He was killing me. "Tonight you're going to be dead."

on the third night the boxer came back to me like Jesus Christ and untied my bonds "let the accused state," he said, "his full name age occupation permanent address because the judge has blond hair he's a German or a germ," giving a tug to the elastic band of his briefs reaching inside bringing forth sticky bubblegum used condoms Mars bars half-sucked lollipops snap crackle pop

"but I can't be a criminal if I'm dead."

"if the accused speaks once more out of turn I'm going to shove his purple tongue backwards up his nostrils so he has to give me a ream job through his nostrils" "your asshole's smellier than my nostrils." I wanted to say this to my accuser, but he was bigger than I was. instead I moaned. "

silence in this court! disrespect will cost the disrespectful! let he who's accused and accused and accused now step forward. hmph. hmph. hmph."

I couldn't step forward cause my legs were still tied up with bubblegum which was unfair *I didn't know my crime*.

"step forward and show the court the hairs in your asshole."

I waited for Tonto to rescue me.

I waited for a long time.

Then it was morning. You said, " I've decided. " You took up my head and put it on your cock. It took you two minutes to dribble a few sperm drops dawn my gullet. "Bye bye."

SOME SORT OF TRIAL

1 child: You can't go. Don't I get a chance to confess? Don't I get a chance to say I'm guilty? Why don't you give me a chance to acknowledge my vicious and mysterious crimes? Can't I be a traitor? Can't I be punished forever? Can't I be an iron chain? I don't know the difference between being punished with iron chains and being an iron chain cause I'm stupid. Won't you fuckin' give me a chance you're so mean.

2 child: No, you can't confess. Wanting to confess to crimes you did and crimes you didn't do doesn't make sense. I care so much about you that what you want, punishment, hurts me.

1 child: But I want to confess. For years, cause I haven't confessed, I've gotten nothing. Cause I haven't confessed, nothing touches me. It isn't fair! Now I'm going to confess to everything . . .

2 child: Do you know what'll happen to you if you confess in court to a serious crime? Death...destruction...pain.

You can't now even watch a needle go into a cat in a film.

1 child: I know. It's horrible. I'm horrible. I'm worse than horrible. I'm evil. But boredom's more boring than evil and you've proven your boringness. So now it's my turn: I'm a pirate and I'm a murderer and I'm running after a man who isn't running after me and laying my body under his feet so he can trample me up and the feminists're watching. And all trampled up by him and his friends, I'll be laying in the piss in the gutter the ocean I don't want to drown glub glub not today maybe tomorrow.

2 child: No matter what dreadful...unimaginable crimes you can confess to, no one's ever going to love you. Do what you want; you'll never get what you want.

1 child: You gonna have to kill me by drowning me in the ocean where there are lots of living and dead sailors all of whom have big things between their legs.

2 child: OK, fatso, now I've heard your confession and you really have convinced me that you're a suppurating pussy if there is any Justice in this court, according to the good oldtime American system of equality and liberalism, you're going to be buried in sand like girls always do to boys. No, first boys try to ignore the existence of girls so the girls try to kiss them. The boys run panic-stricken from female caresses the girls chase them into deeper sands and capture them. That's how girls get back at pirates. You're not really a girl, are you, fatso?

1 child: I'm not fat that's not fair you've got to torture me some other way not by always refusing to give me food I'm sick of not getting any food you're the one who loves not giving anything.

2 child: I don't even remember the subject of this trial. Oh, yes. The subject in front of this court is a sailor who's in love with a man he doesn't know.

1 child: Yes, that's true.

The two children in pajamas, sitting in a bunk, facing each other, made faces at each other and tried to scare each other by throwing the light of flashlights in each other's chins, but only created illusions of skulls.

I saw no way of making them agree.

ALTERATIONS OF REALITY AND CHILDHOOD

As soon as the boxer had come slightly in my mouth, he had said goodbye. I was left alone like an open asshole. I want a cock, a fist up my asshole. I want reality that lies, like everything lies, on the surface of the butcher's shop's table where the cuts of meat stink more than they wait.

I had to transform this situation so that I could deal with it. I had to make my imagination real. I needed the boxer to get my sexuality. People who are absent, like imagined people or dead people, aren't real.

I needed a weapon to fight him. To get him back. To destroy

absence. I knew absence before I was born. I decided to give death a shove where it hurt most.

I remembered that I had lived with a woman. In the sixth year she informed me she was leaving me I said I'd do anything and be anything so she wouldn't leave she left me.

Give death a shove where it hurts the most.

Nothing happens unless it's real. To pit oneself by means of a weapon, muscularity, against death is to have value. For it must be sufficient to transfer to the world of flesh what, since I'm scared, is more safely, more easily done in the imaginative world.

My only weapon against the boxer seemed to be my muscularity. But I had no idea what this muscularity—these muscles which run along the shoulder bones, growing thicker as they reach certain places in the arms, the pecs which easily flex, the tightened buttocks which can allow a greaseless hand to move easily between them—what these well-developed muscles like mad children have to do with another person.

I had no way of reaching the boxer. He had given me neither an address nor a phone number. I had to wait for him to touch me. If he was going to. I find waiting unbearable because it makes me passive and negates me. I hate being nothing. He didn't care about me. A man who didn't care about me was making me nothing. I remembered I had sworn to let no one touch me. Now I decided, if I was going to destroy death, I would have to be dead. I didn't know whether or not the boxer cared about me.

Though suicide's the opposite of muscularity, it's muscularity that allows suicide.

The boxer arrived one night unexpectedly.

"actually you're not a real pussy," he whispered while lying on my belly first he fucked me behind but actually his cock couldn't get hard, "you're an asshole you know why?" maybe he was making himself hard by jerking himself off "cause you're lying on your ass your name is barley raspberry red and twisted candy lemon yellow hole" then he took my mouth and put it to his cock

his cock rigid thick as a candle funny bump in the middle it shoots dripping wax splashes into my mouth then drops out its drool all over the place the mattress on which we're lying's a mess.

as soon as he comes two drips in my mouth then splatters spatters all aver the place he mutters "I'm going to go" which is no fun at all besides he's already done that so I answer "instead of leaving and leaving me to hideous abandonment why don't you instead kill me? if you killed me," I plead sensibly, "I wouldn't feel the hideous abandonment. Just as when the most hideous of Berber chieftains takes a girl who's been masturbating to the point of blood and shoves a prick the size of a goat's into her as-yet-untouched-except-by-her-own-shit one-half-centimeter diameter asshole and she doesn't say anything. She just looks at him. Then he turns her around on his cock. Just so: I want you to kill me so that there'll be no tomorrow."

he says, "OK I'll kill you."

I ask him how "I don't want anything too painful cause pain scares me."

"what do you care about pain when you don't care about death"

"that's not the point"

"what's the point?"

"there's no point to all this"

"then why do you want to die now?"

"cause I can remember pain but I can't remember death" he says convinced though it makes him feel good to hurt me, he cares enough about me to kill me and besides killing me'll be fun

it's good we always get along

now that I've got a daddy, life and death no longer matter then the skin of his face looks like that of an old man because he's become a Nazi he has to be a Nazi now because he's German I'm a sailor his facial skin always becomes old when he's focused

And here it came to me on the path of sexuality… secretly…ambushing me…there was an infatuating warm smell coming from the bare skin, a soft lecherous cajolery. And yet there was something about it so solemn and compelling as to make one almost clap one's heart in awe.

"do you want to eat one last time.?" as if I was really in front of a firing squad and being granted one last request so I asked the Nazi if I could smoke a cigarette, though I don't smoke cigarettes, rather than put one out on my body which I also swore, one day, if he really loved me, I'd do

then I said to the Nazi, "I'm hungry"

"that's because you're about to die a thing like that always makes a guy hungry all those Spanish anarchists were ravenous but they had the discipline not to say so they were sleepy too"

I protested to the Nazi I didn't want to fall asleep cause then I wouldn't know what it is to die and I had only one chance to die you only die for love once then I looked up to him and he was slightly taller than me and asked him what we should do now cause I didn't have any food in the house cause pirating took up too much of my time

"we don't have to do a fuckin' thing we don't we can do whatever we want" he puts thumbs on my throat my cock grows and rubs against his stomach

There was danger now...somewhere...lying in wait...not the open but an ambush...not what seemed to be here...something that would actually tear me, or the me that is memory, apart...This had hard comers and was tangible reality. My eyes awakened out of sleep.

"but do we have to stay here a long time" while I was still able to speak

his thumbs pressed down harder my cock got harder for his thumbs

After I died, the boxer bent down over me. A curve of an eyebrow was all that showed that he had feelings. My flesh was still warm. He lifted a sheet over me, then stretched himself out on top of me under the sheet. For the first time his undressed body was next to mine.

The boxer pressed his bulge into mine. Where mine used to be. Death desexualized. He kissed my forehead while his hard thing plowed exploring into my hole. I screamed from the pain deep inside me. He went wild shooting off into me. He hadn't done that before. He clutched at me, twisted my nipples, tore my face. The myth had become apparent. His fucking cock sounded an opening into my pubis's innominate bone.

I opened my eyes fully and saw the boxer standing on my right, wiping sperm off his cock. The wind from the open sea made both of us shiver. I managed to touch his mouth just as he lay down on me again and pushed his tongue through my closed mouth as no child has ever kissed. "I'm not going to leave you."

THE BIRTH OF THE POET

A PLAY IN THREE ACTS

The Birth of the Poet was first performed at the Brooklyn Academy of Music Next Wave Festival in New York City on December 3, 1985 with the following cast:

Stabbed Arab Lover *Frank Dahill*
Ali/Hinkley *Zach Grenier*
Cynthia *Jan Leslie Harding*
Maecenas *Stuart Hodes*
Shadow from San Francisco *Anne Iobst*
Propertius *Max Jacobs*
Hassidic Book Delivery Man *Warren Keith*
Barbarella *Anne Lange*
Stabbed Arab Wife *Brooke Myers*
Street of Dogs Town Crier *Harsh Nayyar*
Danielle *Ingrid Reffert*
Lady With the Whip *Valda Setterfield*

Director: *Richard Foreman*
Music: *Peter Gordon*
Scenery and Costume Design: *David Salle*
Lighting Design: *Pat Collins*
Sound Design: *Otts Munderloh*

ACT ONE

(The stage looks exactly what New York City looks outside the theater. The middle of a huge nuclear power plant. Dark and cavernous.)

WHITE WW 1: (*i.e., World Worker 1; explaining to a potential worker.*) This factory is the newest of the new.

WHITE WW 2: (*To the same girl.*) Yes. We don't even get paid.

WHITE WW 1: (*Before she can open her mouth.*) Everything is provided for us.

WHITE WW 2: We do everything for ourselves because we're modern.

POTENTIAL WORKER: Oh. (*A limbless White Worker enters.*)

WHITE WW 2: We even hire limbless spasmodics. (*The limbless White Worker is carrying ten-foot-long pipes on his head.*)

WHITE WW 1: The only thing we need to keep going is files. Files of the workers' medical insurance, files of the workers' life insurance, files of the workers' car insurance, files of the workers' theft insurance, files of the workers' fire insurance.

WHITE WW 2: This is the only reason we need workers.

POTENTIAL WORKER: (*Enthusiastic.*) Yah!

WHITE WW 2: Products are out-of-date. No one can afford to buy anyway.

POTENTIAL WORKER: (*or P.O.W.*) What about the Bosses?

WHITE WW 1: They're on salary like the rest of us. The business pays for everything.

WHITE WW 3: (*Talking to a visiting Rich Man who's coked-up.*) We make energy!

WHITE WW 1: Coal is obsolete and dirty. Oil almost brought the world to its knees begging for survival. This new energy will drive millions of new machines forever and ever. We are creating it. Nuclear mixed with solar energy allows the possibility of worldly existence.

WHITE WW 2: We need solid capable workers. We need workers who can understand what we're doing. Who will work harder harder because there is nothing to work for. (*The underground cavern grows darker, areas of shifting hall-light, huge cavernous pillars like the rocks in the ancient Roman days, machines, just huge shapes.*)

WHITE WW 2: Production production continues uninterrupted. We will never again allow a shortage of energy in the modern world.

RICH COKED-UP VISITOR: (*Turning around to White WW 2.*) And what if this place should blow up? (*White WW 2 doesn't answer.*)

WHITE WW 4: (*To White WW 5.*) What d'you want now? We were just betting on the temperature of the air outside.

WHITE WW 5: I got a report from the factory.

WHITE WW 4: Your machine?

WHITE WW 5: Some fission material is missing.

WHITE WW 4: Where?

WHITE WW 5: During the process.

WHITE WW 4: A leak?

WHITE WW 5: Probably a computer mistake.

WHITE WW 4: Has it happened more than once?

WHITE WW 5: I've been watching steadily. For five hours now.

WHITE WW 4: There's nothing wrong with the computer?

WHITE WW 5: (*Slightly panicking.*) I'd better find out.

RICH COKED-UP VISITOR: The world's ending!The world's ending!

(*In a corner of the factory.*)

SHADOW 1: Please love me.

SHADOW 2: I can't love you anymore. I'm pooped.

SHADOW 1: I'm so desperate for you. I've been traveling all over the world. Well, in San Francisco. Being in San Francisco is so boring it's like being everywhere in the world. I've got to have you I'll even brandish a whip to get you.

SHADOW 2: You've never gone that way before.

SHADOW 1: I'm growing up.

RED WW 1: Report from third workshop-production one point below quota.

RED WW 2: Report from fifth workshop-production two points below quota.

RED WW 3: Report from fifth computer-fission leakage up three points.

RED WW 4: Control stations on fourth level register reduced energy production. By performance up to twelve behind target.

RED BOSS: Whose fault is it?

RED WW 1: All computers work perfectly.

RED WW 2: All seismographs work perfectly.

RED WW 3: All cyclotrons work perfectly.

RED WW 4: All Browning effects work perfectly.

(*The Rich Visitor starts taking off his clothes and shits on the floor.*)

BLUE WW 1: Report from first workshop-all alarms sounding.

BLUE WW 2: Report from second workshop—all transport buses racing from their sheds.

BLUE WW 3: All workers while trying to escape under total discipline and time cards.

BLUE WW 4: Steady food supply with generous priorities while collapse of workers at gauge-gear-pedal lever.

BLUE BOSS: Movement becomes autonomous for survival. Excessive duration of the one action stops the body from digesting. Poison piles up.

TRANSLUCENT WW: Power in its essence is in no way material, it has no essence at all in a philosophical sense, and it is an apparently unnameable figment of the imagination.

(*Slowly, the large window glass is cracking. After this cracking sound, all is totally still, suddenly BAM BAM BAM (very rhythmical). Nuclear-solar leakage looks gray and red. The whole stage blows to bits and the play is over.*)

BLACK WW 1: I'll bet ya' the nuclear leakage factor is up fifteen points.

BLACK WW 2: Twenty.

BLACK WW 1: How much?

BLACK WW 2: Ten.

BLACK WW 1: Fuck you. Look at the weather outside. Nothing's wrong there.

(*They all look through the now totally opaque because so shattered and splintered panes of the huge windows.*)

BLACK WW 3: I'll take both of you on for as much as you want that leakage is up fifty points.

BLACK WW 2: What're ya' doing?

BLACK WW 1: I'm calling WEATHER to find out how much nuclear leakage is in the air.

BLACK WW 4: The phone lines aren't working.

(*The squawkings of peacocks kangaroos ostriches and leopards can be heard slightly. The workers fall down dead.*)

LAST WW: Report from control-room: this is the end of the world.

(*There is just rubble and smoke. Out of this rubble rises,*

ACT TWO

I'M THINKING ABOUT YOU RIGHT NOW AND I'VE BEEN
THINKING ABOUT YOU FOR DAYS WHEN I JERK OFF I SEE
YOUR FACE AND I'M NOT GOING TO STOP WRITING THIS
CAUSE THEN I'LL BE AWAY FROM THIS DIRECTNESS THIS
HAPPINESS THIS ISNESS WHICH IS. AT THE SAME TIME I'M
NEVER GOING TO HAVE ANYTHING TO DO WITH YOU AGAIN.
BECAUSE YOU, EVEN IF IT IS JUST CAUSE OF CIRCUM-
STANCES, WON'T LOVE ME. THIS ISN'T THE SITUATION. I'M
BEING A BABY AS USUAL. THERE ARE COMPLICATIONS. ARE
SHADES, HUES, NEVER EITHER-OR, THE SHADES ARE MEAN-
INGS, COME OUT, YOU ROTTEN COCKSUCKER

1. TO THE DOOR

CYNTHIA: (*The whore.*) Why aren't you grabbing my cunt every
chance you get? I love fucking in public streets and why are
you telling me you want to be friends and work with me
more than you care about sex with me, but you don't want
FOR ANY REASONS to cut out the sex? Do you want to own
me without owning me? (*Cynthia leaves to search for
Propertius, her boyfriend. It's night. She finds him.*) Why
don't you take me? I've only got five minutes. Why does it
have to last beyond these grabbing actions. Oh I believe in
love that thing that is impossible to happen. (*A bones-stick-
ing-out cow drags a cart of glittering religious objects past a
dead murderer over the bumpy street.*) And you're fat and
ugly and I'm more beautiful than you and I've got more
money and I can earn more in five minutes in this world: you
should be taking ME out to dinner. Here's a hole the window
we can climb through to where we can fuck.
PROPERTIUS: (*Rubs his cock.*) When I was a kid, I used to use a
bottle with something in it. Now I've got cunts, but cunts
have women attached to them. By Augustus's nose! I'm a
man! The best wet dream I had was in highschool, I was
fucking this girl I desperately wanted to fuck her hole disappeared I still kept shoving rubbing up against her. I woke up
and I was pounding into the bed. Actually I don't want you
to have anything to do with me. I just want split open red
and black pussy.
CYNTHIA: Why don't you let me go? I want to go back to that
non-existing where I can do what I want.

79

PROPERTIUS: I like you a lot. (*Cynthia pisses on Propertius.*)

CYNTHIA: That doesn't work. If I let you make all the decisions, you'll be my father.

PROPERTIUS: I don't want to make any decisions. People tell me what to do very easily and I won't stand being told what to do, so I avoid people.

CYNTHIA: (*Deciding in herself.*) He's never going to give me what I want, but I'll still fuck him. (*They're standing in front of a huge partly opened window behind which is black space.*)

CYNTHIA: O.K. baby. lump- What's the matter with you, are you too fat to jump? I've got five minutes. You're going be a creep and not do anything, I'm scared too, I want it. Flesh is it. Your lips are it.

PROPERTIUS: Isn't that guy on the corner waiting for you?

CYNTHIA: That's why we've got only five minutes.

2. AT A DOOR'S EDGE

(*During the night, these streets very narrow dirty uneven rocks no way to be sure of your footing much less direction as for safety all sorts of criminal or rather people who have to survive hiding under one level of stone or behind an arcade you can't even see just standing there. No way to tell the difference between alive and dead. Criminalities which are understandable mix with religious practices, for people have to do anything to satisfy that which can no longer be satisfied*

We shall define sexuality as all that which can't be satisfied

[*Simultaneous contrasts, extravagances, incoherences, half-formed misshapen thoughts, lousy spellings.*]

Elegance and completely filthy sex fit together. Expectations which can't be satiated.)

CYNTHIA: Just why are you fucking me? You've got a girlfriend named Trick and you love her. According to you, she's satisfied with you and you with her. (*Propertius is staring blankly at the door.*) I'm sick of being nice to you. So what if you want a girl who'll consider you her top priority and yet'll never ask you for anything? I can't be her. (*Propertius is staring blankly at the door and scratching his head.*) DON'T FUCK ME CAUSE YOU LIKE MY WORK. LEAVE ME ALONE. This is the only way I can directly speak to you cause you're autistic.

PROPERTIUS:

Oh little cunt door

I love you so very very much.

CYNTHIA: Well, everyone wants to fuck me so I tell you I'm sick of this life. Who cares if you're another person waiting at my door. You're just another man and you don't mean shit to me.

PROPERTIUS: Please, cunt, I'm cold and I'll be the best man for you. I know you're fucking someone else that's why you won't let me near you. You cheap rags stinking fish who wants anything to to with corpses anyway? (*To himself.*) And thus I tried to drown my mourning.

CYNTHIA: This is the door out I want, goddamn you. Now I'm dead: I want

One. My mother father and grandmother are dead. Fuck that.

Two. When my mother popped off, afterwards, she lay in this highly polished wood coffin in the most expensive funeral house in New York City-where all the society dk after they're dead-FAKE, everything was real but there are times real is fake, flowers, tons of smells, wood halls polished like fingernails, rabbi or preacher asks me, "Do you know anything good I can say (you have to say something: SAY SOMETHING!) over your mother's mutilating body?" (it being understood that all society people are such pigs that) and I tell him how beautiful she is; no one cries they're there to stare at me as I make my blind way through the narrow aisle to number how hysterical I am did I really love her? The beginning of the funeral: the family lawyer, having walked over to me, shakes my lapels,

"Where are the 800 IBM shares?" "What 800 IBM shares?" "There are 800 missing IBM shares and no one knows how your mother died. I thought she might have given them to you." "She never gave me a penny."

Three. I do everything for sexual love. What a life it's like I no longer exist cause no one loves me. So *when I die*, I'll die because you'll know *that you caused me to die* and you'll be responsible. That's what my death'll do to you and you'll learn to love. I'm teaching you by killing myself.

Four. You're gonna have to die too. You'll be like me. You'll be where I now am. Your cock-bone will lie in my cunt-bone.

Five. This is why life shits: because you're gonna love me the second I leave you flat. Sexuality comes from repression. In the long run, nothing matters. This is the one sentiment that makes me happy.

Please be nice to me.

BARBARELLA: You've got to own a man who has money.

DANIELLE: I want money and power.

CYNTHIA & BARBARELLA: (*Agreeing.*) Money and sex are definitely the main criteria.

DANIELLE: Sex?

CYNTHIA: I think I want a wife who has a cock. You understand what I mean. I don't understand why men even try to deal with me like I can be a wife, and then bitch at me and hurt me as much as possible cause I'm not. Who'd ever think I'm a wife? Do you think I'm a wife? (*Barbarella giggles.*) But when I'm sexually open, I totally change and this real fem part comes out.

BARBARELLA: I want a husband. No. I take that back. I want someone who'll support me.

CYNTHIA: Good luck.

BARBARELLA: I'm both the husband and wife. Even though none of us is getting anything right now, except for Danielle who's getting everything, our desires are totally volatile.

DANIELLE: I can't be a wife. I can be a hostess. If I've got lots of money.

CYNTHIA: I think if you really worship sex, you don't fuck around. Danielle fucks around more than any of us and she's the one who doesn't care about sex.

BARBARELLA: Most men don't like sex. They like being powerful and when you have good sex you lose all power.

CYNTHIA: I need sex to stay alive.

(*A street in Rome. The sky's color is deep dark blue. One star can be seen. Very little can be seen on this street-just different shades of black.*)

3. INSIDE

Now we're fucking:

I don't have any finesse I'm all over you like a raging blonde leopard and I want to go more raging I want to go snarling and poisoning and teasing eek eek, curl around your hind leg pee, that twig over there, I want your specific piss shuddering out of your cock. I want you to help me. I need help.

Take off your clothes. Clothes imprison. Clothes imprison legs and mouths and red teeth still shudder want too much, taking off our clothes,

Why can't you ever once do something that's not allowable? I mean goddamnit.

Hit me.

Do anything.

Do something.

Sow this hideousness opposition blood to everyone proud I want to knock Ken over with a green glass I want to hire a punk to beat up Pam I will poison your milk if you don't have your girlfriend.

Sex is public. The streets made themselves for us to walk naked down them. Take out your cock and piss over me.

The threshold is here. Commit yourself to not-knowing. Legs lie against legs. Hairs mixing hairs and here, a fingerpad, a space, a hand, a space, hairs mixed with hairs.

Go over this threshold with me.

Thumb, your two fingers pinch my nipples while your master bears down on me. Red eyes, stare down on the top of my eyes. Cock, my eyes are staring at you pull out of the brown hairs. Red eyes, now you're watching your cock pull out of the strange brown hairs. Thumb, your two fingers pinch my nipples while your master bears down on me.

Now you've gone away:

Joel whom I thought hated me saw me every other day and Rudy whom I thought the worst that is the meanest of my boyfriends always called me every other day or let me call him and I don't know reality. Peter who lives with another girl three thousand miles away from me and he adores her phones me at least once a month.

This guy obviously doesn't care about me.

But when he looks at me, I know there's a hole in him he loves me. No he doesn't. I can't do anything in the world until I know whether he loves me or not. I have to learn whether he loves me or not.

You might just as well accept you're in love with him because if you give him up just cause he doesn't adore you enough, you'll have nothing. In the other case, there's a one percent chance you'll keep touching his flesh.

CYNTHIA, sitting at her dressing-table in her little apartment overlooking the middleclass Roman whores' section, is dressing her hair: That goddamn son-of-a-bitch I hope he goes to hell I hope he gets POISONED wild city DOGS should drive their thousands of TEETH-FANGS through his flesh a twelve-year old syphilitic named Janey Smith should wrap her cunt around that prick I hate that prick those fingers I hate black hair I want his teeth to rip themselves out in total agony I want his lips to dry up in Grand Canyon gulfs I want him PARALYZED never to be able to move again and to be conscious of it:

Now, louse, you'll learn. You'll learn what it is not to know. I want you to learn what it is to want like fire. The driest and coldest dry ice: the top of your head will burn and the rest of your body will freeze shake muscles will cramp as they do when they're not yet used to the bedless floor, at night, you will know agony.

You must learn what it is to want.

I'm a whore who's unable to hold in and repress her emotions.

Propertius decides he doesn't want to fuck Cynthia again: How can such a stinking fish, a cunt who has experienced what it is to be the wish-fulfillment of many men, hordes of men, more men than promote the Great Caesar, be innocent? Moreover she's had such a poverty-regulated life, she can't have the life in her to give me the female elegance and beauty I deserve.

My girlfriend on the other hand, if anyone ever hurts me, is going to have to murder him. For me. When I'm dying from a worn out liver punctured guts three punches in the face and dirty track marks because I've lived life to the hilt, my girlfriend will commit suicide.

As a whore, Cynthia goes from man to man because she's no man's possession. So there's no possibility I'm going to love her and, if I fuck her, it's just cause she's an open cunt. Women's libbers are right when they want to get rid of all you whores by locking you up.

CYNTHIA: I've been waiting for you.
PROPERTIUS: What the he...(*Grabbing the other girl into him.*)
    Oh, hello. I'm busy now.
CYNTHIA: I just wanted to see you.
PROPERTIUS: I'm busy with someone now. I'll give you a call tomorrow.
CYNTHIA: Please. (*There's nothing she can do.*) O.K. (*Propertius*

and his girlfriend walk into the house. One of the dogs on the street starts barking.)

The street of Dogs. Two lines of houses lead to a Renaissance perspective. These lines are seemingly only-surface connected three-story townhouses. A sun and a three quarter moon hang fakely over one townhouse. Common household objects such as lamps, a part of a table, half of a torn plastic rose kitchen curtain take up some of the window space. Outside a townhouse, a dog leans over her basket of laundry. Two dogs, one leaning farther out its window than the other, open their mouths to howl. Their teeth are sharp and white and they have very long red tongues. One dog over her basket of wash gossips with another dog. Two young dogs are mangling each other next to the curb. On each side of the street the tall thin windows form a long row.

CYNTHIA: *(Barks like a dog.)* I can't help myself anymore I'm just a girl I didn't ask God to be born a girl. If I think realistically, I know I'm an alien existant. I hate everyone in the world. But I can't think. You're just so cute. I have to get you out of my body because you're a disease. I don't want to and why should 171 want this sweet thing that is you. I'm going to go after you, aching sore, a don't care what your reaction is to me), because why not, darling.

(Cynthia walks up to Propertius's door and sits in front of it. The door doesn't move.)

(A big bald-headed man opens the door lays his palms on the doorway. Cynthia goes away.)

You alone born from my most beautiful carecure for grief
Shuts out since your fate "COME OFTEN HERE"
Fiction by my will will become the most popular form
Propertius, your forgiveness, peace, Peter, yours.
to redefine the realms of sex so sex
I'm crawling up the wall for you.
                          I must face facts I'm not a
female. I must face facts I can't be loved. I must
face facts I need love to live. Hello, walls.
How're you doing today? Hello, my watch. Please watch
over Propertius, you are here because I will
never get near him again. He is now forbidden
territory.

(Cynthia lies down on the street and sticks razor blades up her arms. The bums ask her if she needs a drink.)

CYNTHIA: Madness makes an alcoholic sober, keeps the most raging beast in an invisibly locked invisible cage, turns seething masses of smoke air calm white, takes a junky off junk as if he's having a pleasant dream, halts that need FAME that's impossible.

I am only an obsession. Don't talk to me otherwise. Don't know me. Do you think I exist?

Watch out. Madness is a reality, not a perversion.

Among these women, free yet timorous, addicted to late hours darkened rooms gambling indolence, sparing of words, all they needed was an allusion.

I reveled in the quickness of their half-spoken threats more like the violent excitement of a teenager who doesn't know what he feels. These exchanges as if once the slow-thinking male is banished every message from woman to woman is clear and overwhelming are few in kind and infallible.

The first time I dined at her place, three brown tapers dripped waxen tears in tall candlesticks without dispelling the gloom. A low table, from the Orient, offered a pell-mell of les hors d'oeurve-strips of raw fish rolled upon glass wands, foie gras, shrimps, salad seasoned with pepper and cranberry-there was a well-chosen Piper Heidsieck brut and very strong Russian Greek and Chinese alcohols. I didn't believe I'd become friends with this woman who tossed off her drink with the obliviousness with which a person in the depths of opium watches his hand burn.

The "master" is never referred to by the name of woman. We seemed to be waiting for some catastrophe to project herself into our midst, but she merely kept sending invisible messengers laden with jades, enamels, lacquers, furs...From one marvel to another...Who is the dark origin of all this nonsense?

"Tell me, Renèe. Are you happy?

Renèe blushed, smiled, then abruptly stiffened.

"Why, of course, my dear Colette. Why would you want me to be unhappy?"

"I didn't say I wanted it," I retorted.

"I'm happy," Renèe explained to me, "but the sexual ecstasy is so great, I'm going to be physically sick."

PROPERTIUS: If you read every poem in every anthology of Greek
poetry, you wouldn't read one poem in which the character
of the woman who's loved is described or matters.

That's cause women are goddamn sluts. They're goddamn
sluts because the only thing they've got going for them are
their cunts.

The worse thing about women is all these emotions. Take
the hole I slept with last night. Sure, she moaned hard when
I stuck my dick in her. But did she have any idea that I didn't
feel? Sure, I'm a macho pig. Why should I pre tend I'm something I'm not I care about art. Everything but art is a second-
class existent.

Art, you are the black hole of vulnerability, you take everything from me and are not human. You can take me whenever you want me. A human has to care for one thing.

I use whatever I can get from women. I maul the need they
offer me. I increase their anguish or insecurity and horniness
to elephantine proportions. So the ugly is left ugly and consciousness' unavoidable anguish is as it is in me.

My writing will cure you of your suffering. I teach young girls
how to win the love of men who don't love them. I teach
boys how to endure the lacerations of long red fingernails
stuck in their face flesh and how to watch the girl they crawl
under fuck another man right in front of their faces.

AUGUSTUS: (*Through the lips of his literary counselor
Maecenas.*) You're not a poet and you're not a real man
because you write about emotion. Men are people who take
care of the world, who care that people get enough to eat,
who stop the greedy hawks at least from seizing more power
and underhanded control.

Artists who are men have to change the world. When they
start paying attention to emotions, what are emotions?,
they're helping the power hawks destroy the social bonds
people need to live.

PROPERTIUS: Then my writing destroys social bonds so that's
who I am.

MAECENAS: You're speaking stupidly, pettily, and you're too
smart to take this position. Writing is not about egotism.

PROPERTIUS: One day, Maecenas, you're going to realize you're
not rational and then, suddenly ignorant desperate, you'll

leave your politics and run to me, (*Turns away from Maecenas.*) away from anything public, the art-world: a salon resplendent with gilding and illuminations. One has just revealed original talent and with this first portrait of his shows himself the equal of his teacher. A sculptor's chatting with one of those clever satirists who refuse to recognize merit and think they're smarter than anyone else. The people talk either about how they earn money or who's becoming famous. All for good reason are grasping. Since the only ideas are for sale, none are mentioned. A few women are existing to maintain the surface that heterosexuality is still conceivable. Eyes never see
mouths faces are talking to
away from the art-world,

You can say I write stories about sex and violence, with sex and violence and therefore my writing isn't worth considering because it uses content much less lots of content and all the middle-range people or moralists say I'm a disgusting violent sadist. Well, I tell you this:
Prickly race,
who know nothing except how to eat out your own hearts with envy, you don't eat cunt,
writing isn't a viable phenomenon anymore. Everything has been said. All these lines aren't my writing: Philetas's Demeter far outweighs his long old woman, and of the two, it's his little pieces of shit I applaud. May the crane-who-delights-in-the-Pygmies'-blood's flight from Egypt to Thrace be so long, like me in your arms, endless endless grayness, may the death shots the Massagetae're directing against a Mede be so far: what is here: desire violence will never stop. Go die off, you, you destructive race of the Evil Eye, or learn to judge poetic appearance by art: art is the elaborating of violence. Don't look to me to want to change the world. I'm out of it.

But if there hadn't been between you the two the dark streets, the risks, and the old man you had just abandoned, had there been no danger, would you have hurried so eager-ly?

PROPERTIUS: (*To Cynthia who isn't in front of him.*) I know
you've been going through hell because I've been refusing to
speak to you.

    I know the moment I stopped talking to you, you slit
your wrist (you did that just cause when you were in your
teens you regularly cut your arms with a razor blade to show
yourself you were horror), then more seriously you got an
ovarian infection because your ovaries had been rejected.
You tried I know you tried you did avoid me (except when
you phoned ten times a day, my girlfriend answered the
phone and you hung up).

    Listen, Cynthia. I fucked so many girls I took them up to
this penthouse sauna and swimming pool someone had lent
me. Beautiful girls pass each other on the stairway. Limbs
disappear in the shadow, and there's nothing else.

(*About his new girlfriend to Cynthia who isn't in front of him.*)
The more I knew she was fucking every man she'd meet through
me, the more I'd do anything for her-crazed because I knew every
move she made was part of her leaving me. Then it stopped; she
ran away with her other boyfriend.

    I want you, Cynthia.

    If you don't give your total flesh and everything else
over to me, slimy bitch, may you drink raw oyster-like
blood—you now living on your dead grandmothers capitalis-
tic hoard-may whatever food your lips and smell come near
stink of shit-filled guts, human, always always you regret
everything you seem to yourself to be. Your thoughts are
wild fantasies. Wild fantasies eat you, hole. Looking everywhere looking everywhere looking everywhere looking
everywhere: each human is so stupid it's a ravenous wolf.
Long red pointed fingernails will separate the cunt lip flesh,
then dig into the soft purple, and around the protrusion of
the nipple right there, another fingernail.

    This is why you can't run away from me. There's only
obsession.

    Love will turn on the lover and gnaw.

(*On his knees, to Cynthia who isn't in front of him.*) Last night I
had this dream, Cynthia. You stood over me. The ring I had given

you, your finger, the white palm outstretched. You said these following words to me:

CYNTHIA: I didn't mean to tell you your girlfriend was fucking around, but (1) you had just told me I wasn't a female because I have a "career" and because I'm not a female no man will love me. That hurt. (2) You set up the terms of the relationship, but I was thinking about you all the time so you said STAY RATIONAL but I wasn't rational: this was confusing me. I explained my identity-desperation by telling you I had known your girlfriend was two-timing you that's why I let myself love you. But the second I mentioned the first word, explosion!, so I backed off: I just heard gossip, the gossip was old she wasn't fucking anyone else. I'm wrong to listen to gossip. Let me be hurt. (3) I said "Propertius is no more," but my body reacted: I cut a razor blade through my flesh so I could see the flesh hole revealing two thin purple-bluegray wires which frightened and reminded me of my mother's chin three days after she committed suicide, the body gets sick. I'm not a woman who takes shit, but
        Why do I like you so much? I like you you so much you're necessary to the continuing of my existence right now and I don't understand this at all, I just know it's true.

PROPERTIUS: Cynthia walked away from me, and I woke up. (*To Cynthia who isn't in front of him.*) I don't want you, slut, because desire is mad and I don't want to be mad.

ACT THREE

ALI GOES TO THE MOSQUE
(AT FIRST THERE IS ONLY LANGUAGE AND NOTHING ELSE.)

آیا بازار دور آست؟ نخیر ،خانم،
سرخ نیست دل مرگ آست

Aya hzar dur ast? Naxeir, xanom, sorx nist vali marg ast.
Is the bazaar far? No, Mrs., it's not red it's dead.

نیز میوه هست

Niz mive hast.
There's fruit too.

بازار بسیار زیباست

Bazar besiar ziba st.
The bazaar is very beautiful.

90

Aya mive sorx ast?
Is the fruit red?

آیا میوه سرخ است؟

Bali, xanom, xeili gran ast.
Yes, Mrs., it's very expensive.

بلی، خانم، خیلی گران است

Magar in gusht morde nist?
Isn't this meat dead?

مگر این گوشت مرده نیست؟

Naxeir, xanom, morde nist.
No, Mrs., it isn't dead.

نخیر، خانم، مرده نیست

Aya bank dar in bazar hast?
Is there a bank in this bazaar?

آیا بانک در این بازار هست؟

Bati, xanom, sorx ast.
Yes, Mrs., it is red.

بلی، خانم، سرخ است

Aya mardan hast?
Are there males?

آیا مرداد هست؟

(THE ARAB WOMAN'S SONG FOR HER LOVER WHO IS FAR
FROM HER.)

با حسِّ بینهایتِ والدین و بتنفرِ بی انتهای
اجتماع پرورده بی دردهای ودّاد همیشه است؟

Aya hesse beneferate valedein va betanaffore bi entehae
ejtema' parvarde bi dardhae vedad hamishe ast?
Is feeling fed on parental distaste forever social disdain
always without the pangs of love?

با خود از سرشت دشمنِ جاودانِ ودّاد ام؟

Aya xod az seresht doshmane javadane vedad am?
Am I by nature the lifelong enemy of love?

دالانها چون زندانها و محکمه‌ها:

Dalanha cun zendanha va mahkameha
The labyrinth

کوههای قاتلان

Kuihaye qatelan

91

Alleyways of murderers

Aya hamishe tanha am?
Am I always alone?

آیا همیشه تنها اَم؟

Las
Bitch

لاس

Talxi
Bitterness

تلخ

Beto hame cizra miguyuam
I tell you everything

بِتُو همه چیزرا میگویم

vali zabanra nadaram
but I don't have a tongue.

ولی زبانرا ندارُم

Tab'id xosh ast.
Banishment is pleasant.

تبعید خوش است

Beruye xod ruye mara beband
Link my face to your face

بروی خُود روی مَرا بِبَند

Farar az zaleman mojaz ast.
Flight from tyrants is O.K.

فرار از ظالمان مُجار است

Zaleman ki st?
Who are the tyrants?

ظالمان کیست؟

safar az vos'athaye goh,
traveling through realms of garbage

سَفَر از وُسعَتهای گُه،

otumobile morde hast
"There's a car wreck."

اتومبیل مُرده هست.

Xarcange daraxshan be portoqali
A phosphorescent crab

خَرچنگِ درخشان بپرتقالی

Valedeine xodra hrar mikonim.
We're fleeing our parents.

ولدِینِ خودرا فرار میکنیم.

Xateranaman namidanim.
Our minds don't know.

خاطِرائمان نمیدانم.

Toye koudan, beto
'asheq namibashad.
You dummy, he doesn't love you.

تو کُدُ'ن، بتُو عاشِق نمیباشَد.

To inqadr qarib i: hickas beto
'asheq namibashad.
You're such a freak: no one loves you.

تو اینقَدر قریب ای: هیچکس
بتُو عاشِق نمیباشَد.

Shahrhaye 'arabi qaribanra
dust nadarand.
The Arab cities don't like strangers.

شهرهای عَرَبی غریبانرا دوست ندارند.

Qaribi 'asheqe mara kosht.
A monster has killed my love.

غریبی عاشِقِ مَرا کشت.

ksme morde'e 'asheqe xodra mibinam.
I see my lover's dead body.

جِسم مُردهٔ عاشِقِ خودرا میبینَم.

Hanuz aqabe u mijuyam.
I'm still looking for him.

هنوز عَقَبِ او میجویَم.

Man dar zendegye dardi miayam.
I come in a life of pain.

مَن دَر زِندِگیِ دَردی می آیَم.

(IT'S POSSIBLE TO SEE THE STAGE.)

Xeyabanha xeili seyah inja st.
The streets here are very black.

خِیابانها خیلی سیاه اینجاست

Dalanhaye zendanha va mahkameha
The labyrinth

دالانهای زِندانها وَ مُحکَمهها

این اِرتِفاع
This height

آد فُرهَنگِستان
That academy

بُرجها
Towers for exposing the dead

مُرتَجِع با کَرد

93

Square or round

بی دَر

No door

بی طَرّاحان

No draughtsmen

باز تنگ

Open closed

محل سَرگَشتر

Obelisk refractory

شَهر بی پایان است

The city's endless

نقشه صاف نیست

The map isn't clear

این عمارَت گود است

The building is deep.

آن کوچه ساکت است

An kuce saket ast.
That street is still.

سفیدی هَرجاست

Sefidi harja st.
Whiteness is all-over.

عمارَتها شکل مُنَظّم ریاضیست

'Emaratha shekle monazzame riazist.
The buildings are regular mathematical shapes.

ن عمارَت آبی دادسَراست

An 'emarate abi dadsara'ist.
That blue building is a courthouse.

پیچهای پَستَر رُوشَن نیست

Pichaye pasttar roushan nist.
The lower corners aren't light.

پلّکان بالا میرَوَد

Pelkkan bala miravad.
The steps rise.

پلّکان تاریک نیست

Pellekan tarik nist.
The steps aren't dark.

94

Sahnhaye asman baz ast.
The sky's courtyards're open.

سَحنهای آسمان باز است

Tiz ast.
It is sharp.

تیز است

In mard bi maqz ast.
This man's lobotomized.

این مَرد بی مُغز است

Maqz ra koshtan xeili bad ast.
Lobotomy is horrible.

مُغز را کُشتن خیلی بد است

In mard 'Ali ostadi st.
This man, Ali, is an artist.

این مَرد علی اُستادیست

Kucek va lalimi st.
He's small and Jewish.

کوچک و کَلیمیست

In Yahudian bi maqzan and.
These Jews have no minds.

این یُهودیان بی مُغزان اند

An juxe shahr kalimi st.
That ghetto is Jewish.

آن جوخهٔ شهر کلیمیست

'Arabi tahudi st.
An Arab is a Jew.

عَرَبی یَهودیست

'Ali javan ast vali madarash pir.
Ali is young but his mother's old.

علی جوان است ولی مادَرش پیر

Ali mifahmad an kuce quarib v 'ajib ast.
Ali senses, that street is strange and wonderful.

علی میفهمَد آن کوچه غَریب و عَجیب است

Ketabforushye kalimi qalil ast.
The Jewish bookstore is small.

کِتابفُروشی کَلیمی قَلیل اس

Aya yahudian az 'araban
bahushtar and?
Are Jews more educated than Arabs?

یا یُهودیان از عَرَبان باهوشتَر اند ؟

In so'alha 'Ali ra dard mikonad.
These questions pain Ali.
Ali writes a letter to his mommy,

این سؤالها عَلیرا دَرد میکُند

The day of Reagan's

95

Dear Mom,

Your guts stink. I hate your hair. You must be an Arab cause you have such a large nose. All Arabs are without intelligence. You don't understand my personality because I don't have a personality: I am shifty sneaky devious worthless anonymous wormlike and you've been looking for a real assassin. You want your son to be someone: to grow up and rip out people's guts for money or send poor people to jail for money or tell people all of whom listen what reality is. I'm just like everyone else.

Smelling your flesh when you are with me is agony because you do not love me. We are so different we should hate each other and besides you're a powermonger like all Arabs. We are so unlike each other, mom, even though we fuck, the universe must have been totally sick when it made us. The universe must be totally sick to make us, the two of us, the same blood.

We are going to have to kill each other because there is no other way out of this relationship.

I am banging open my head against my livingroom wall. Any pain helps soften the dry ice needles surrounding and stabbing my right eye swelling up the soft gush around my appendix squeeze my sex muscles into tiny steel pins your presence causes me.

I think you're a real good person and I wouldn't shoot anyone else, I only shot you cause everyone in the world hates you. I do what anyone wants me to. This is the agony. I can't be real anymore. I can't be- much less who- not even what I want. I am total powerlessness. What do you know about agony? I had to shoot you. Everyone knows everything about total agony and the whole world is writhing.

Are we supposed to have sex, mom, even though you're dead?

Your son,

Ali Warnock Hinkley, Jr.

Ali Warnock Hinkley, Jr.

'Ali so'al mikonad masjed ra koja st?   کی سؤال میکند مسجد را کجاست ؟
Ali asks, Where is the mosque?

Ketabforush pasox midehad, naxeir,
pasare motaqalleb, an kuce nist, in ast.
The bookstore man replies,
No, creepy boy, it is not that sidestreet, it is this sidestreet.

كتابفروش پاسخ میدهد، نخیر، پسر
متقلّب، آن کوچه نیست، این آست

Masjed mohemm ast.
The mosque is important.

مسجد مهم آست

Anja azadi hast.
There, there is freedom.

آنجا آزادو هست

Magar in azadi xeili geran nist?
Isn't this freedom very expensive?

مگر این آزادو خیل گران نیست ؟

'Ali tue bazare gusht miravad.
Ali goes into the meat market.

علی توو بازار گوشت میرود

Qachaye bazuyan va payan hast.
There are cut-off arms and legs.

قاچهاو بازویان و پایان هست

Qatele bazuyan va payan kist?
Who is the cutter-off of arms and legs?

قاتل بازویان و پایان کیست ؟

Aya in xeyaban bala miravad?
Is this street climbing upwards?

ایا این خیاباد بالا میرود ؟

Bali, va zard ast.
Yes, and it is pale.

بلی، و زرد آست

Aya yahudi ya 'Arabi
ya qatele siasi hastid?
Are you a Jew, an Arab, or a terrorist?

یا یهودی یا عربی یا قاتل سیاس هستید؟

Inja cizhaye xali faqat hast.
Here is just emptiness.

اینجا چیزهای خالی فقط هست

Aya in 'emarat masjed ast?
Is this building the mosque?

یا این عمارت مسجد آست؟

In 'emrat baz nist.
This building is closed.

این عمارت باز نیست

Markaziat nist. Fekrha nist.
'Aqebatha nist. Entezarha nist.
There is no centralization. There are no thoughts.
There are no goals. There aren't expectations.

بُرکزیّت نیست. فِکرها نیست. عاوِبَتها
بِست. اِنتِظارها نیست.

'Harj o marj qesmate jang ast.
Anarchy is part of war.

هُرج و مُرج قِسمَتِ جَنگ اَست

In bacce dozdi st.
The child is a blackmailer.

اِین بُچّه د'ردیست

In baccegan siah and.
These children are black.

اِین بُچِّگان سیاه آند

Dozdane baxil or haris o darazdast az tavallod va heqarate
tamame mardome birun va xelafe hokumat
Avaricious, rapacious, predatory, born free-booters, hate
strangers, intolerant of restraint

':زدانِ بَخِیلُوحَرِیص 'و د'رازد'ست آز
تَوَ'لّد و حِقارَتِ تَمام مُرد'م بیرون و
خِلافِ حُکومَت

During the days following the assassination of the Archduke
Ferdinand at Sarajevo, people evolved new-because everything is
being destroyed every second-usable languages including noise
distortion lies destruction no language. So today, humans are at
the point of being catatonic and evolving new languages.

Just as post World War I humans had Lenin and Freud, we have
people who are making the most basic processes of human mentality and we don't need anything old.

We are no longer hierarchical. We no longer need men. We
prefer deviation anomie anomaly shift fiction to rules and names.
The repeating noise-making ridiculous functions of language are
more pleasurable when mixed with the expressing ones.

A. In times of war all times we are warriors.

Harj o marj qesmate jang ast.
Anarchy is part of war.

هُرج 'و مُرج قِسمَتِ جَنگ اَست

In balaxane'e bolandi st.
This is a high grating.

اِین باالخانهٔ بُلَندیست

Inja doxtare 'Arabi istad.
An Arab woman stood here.

ینجا دُختَر عَرَبی ایستاد

Pa'in dame mardi naqah kard.
She looked down at a man.

پائین دَمِ مردی نِگاه کَرد

Shouhare 'Arabiash ura kosht.
Her Arab husband stabbed her.

شُوهَر عَرَبیَش اورا کُشت

Houze bozorgye xuni hast.
There was a large pool of blood.

حُوضِ بُزُرگی خون هَست

Aya doxtare 'Arabi zende ast?
Is the Arab woman alive?

یا دُختَر عَرَبی زِنده است

Doxtar morde nist vali hasad zende.
The woman isn't dead, but jealousy is alive.

دُختَر مُرده نیست، وَلی حَسَد زِنده:

زیارَتی تِه مَسجِد

Ziaati te mal'jed
A VISIT TO THE MOSQUE

Ali dare masjedra zad.
Ali knocked on the door of the mosque.

عَلی دَرِ مَسجِدرا زَد

Ranje xodra taslim kard.
He brought his anguish.

رَنجِ خودرا تَسلیم کَرد

Daxele masjed cay va shirini
ra mixorand.
In the mosque they drink tea and sweets.

داخِلِ مَسجِد چای وَ شیرینی را
میخورَند

'Ali goft
Ali said

عَلی گُفت [1]

Inja sagi hast.
Here is a dog.

اینجا سَگی هَست

Inja gorbe' hast.
Here is a cat.

اینجا گُربه هَست

99

Inja zendegi nist.
Here there is no life.

اینجا زندگی نیست

Hic ciz ra namikoni
You don't do anything.

هیچ چیز را نمیکنی

Tanbal i.
You're lazy.

تنبل ئی

Be hic ciz 'aqide daram.
I don't believe anything.

به هیچ چیز عقیده دارم

Dar jahanye 'aquidegan namiziam.
I don't live in a world of belief.

در جهانِ عقیدگان نمیزیم

Bashari az jahan hic ciz ra kay yaft?
When has a human gotten anything from the world?

بشری از جهان هیچ چیز را کی یافت ؟

Shah o pedar ra nadaram v az
hame kas nefrat daram va man xelafe xod mijangam.
I have no king no father I hate everyone
and I'm in continuous war against the self.

شاه و پدر را ندارم و از همه کس نفرت
دارم و من خلافِ خود میجنگم

Har ciz ra miguyam: hickas dar
har surat in zaban ra nadanad.
I say anything no one knows this language anyway.

هر چیز را میگویم : هیچکس در هر صورت
این زبان را نداند

Jense mo'annasam beto baz ast.
My vagina is open to you.

جنسِ مؤنثم بتو باز است

knse mo'annasam dame dastat
ast.
My vagina is at your hand.

جنسِ مؤنثم دمِ دستت است

Muyam dame dastat ast.
My hair is at your hand.

مویم دمِ دستت است

Nefrat to jense mozakkaram
nistid.
You are not my cock, hatred.

نفرت، تو جنسِ مذکرم نالکترم نیستید

100

Jense mo'annasam dar bazar
tazetarin gusht ast va dasti.
My vagina is the freshest meat in the market and a hand.

جنسِ مؤنثَم دَر بازار تازِترین گوشت
ست و دَسی

Jense mo'annasam dar jahan
siahtarin goh ast.
My vagina is the blackest shit in the world.

جِنسِ مؤنثَم دَر جَهان سیاهتَرین گُه است

Maqze man ateshi st.
My brain is a fire.

مَغزِ مَن آتِشیست

Faryad mikonam.
I'm screaming.

فَریاد میکُنَم

Masjed tekke'e goh' ast.
The mosque is a piece of shit.

مَسجِد تِکّهٔ گُه است

Zabane faqate momkenam
'ahirrahaiiiii st.
My only possible speech is 'ahirrahaiiiii.

زَبانِ فَقَط مُمکِنَم عْهِرِّهاهیییست

To xodkoshyam i.
You're my suicide.

تُو خُودکُشیَم ای

_ bad bu darad.
Allah stinks.

الله بَد بو دارِد

ALI GOES TO A WITCH

Dar ya's va jahel 'Ali
be vasileye ketabe loqate
telefun aqabe zane jadu'i
migradat.
In desperation because not knowing anything,
Ali looks through the phone directory for a witch.

دَر یأس و جاهِل عَلی بِوسیلهٔ کِتابِ لُغَتِ
تِلِفون عَقَبِ زَنِ جادوئی میگردد.

Zane jadu baradare
xodra mijavid.
The witch was gnawing on her brother.

زَنِ جادو بَرادَرِ خُود را میجَوید.

101

'Ali bezane jadu goft,
Ali said to the witch,

علی بزن در جادو گفت،

Tanha, mo'allem, tanha va
mast be nefrat o xonak;
Alone, Mistress, alone, drunk on disgust and boring;

تنها، معلّم، تنها و مست به نفرت و خنک؛

Tanha: pesar ba ayande bala
zaxm tolu' nakarde ast;
Alone: the son with expectation hasn't risen above the wound;

تنها: پسر با آینده بالا زخم طلوع نکرده ست؛

Tanha, vali farvardin
az daryaye tarik nure xod
ra midaraxshad
Alone, but Farvardin is glowing its light through the dark sea

تنها، ولی فروردین از دریای تاریک نور خود را میدرخشد

Va vos'ate abi musiqye xun ast
zohre suzesh ast
And blue space is rock-n-roll is burning noon

و وسعت آبی موسیقی خون است زهره سوزش است

Vos'ate avizan karde
ba nabzhaye golhaye
anduxte hame ja.
Space all around hung with pulsating, heaped-up roses.

وسعت آویزان کرده با نبضهای گلهای اندوخته همه جا.

Dar baqha bar baqha bar ruye baqha.
Gardens upon gardens upon gardens.

در باغها بر باغها بر روی باغها

Beyak gol neshan bedeh
Point to one rose

بیک گل نشان بده

Gol jense mo'annas ast.
Gol taryak ast.
The rose is a cunt. The rose is opium.

گل جنس مؤنث است. گل تریاک است.

Tanha, zamestan mo'allem,
be yakdigar vahshate sard
faqat ra ziarat karde
Alone, Winter Mistress, having visited only cold horror on each
other

تنها، زمستان معلّم، به یکدیگر وحشت سرد فقط را زیارت کرده

Ya pedar ya baradar ra nadaram.

یا پدر یا برادر را ندارم.

I have no father no brother.

Man male ya hic hasad ya hic
qazab ya hic sanduq nistam;
I don't belong to any envy or anger or box;

تن مالِ یا هیچ حسد یا هیچ غضب
ا هیچ صُندوق نیستم؛

Har kas mara tark karde ast;
daxele mamlovvye xabha zendegi mikonam,
Everyone has left me: I'm living in the fullness of dreams,

ثر کَس مُرا تَرک کَرده است: داخلِ
مَملُوِّ خوابها زندِگی میکُنَم،

Miane xod va jense
mo'annasi xishi va
'eshq ra Icedmat karde am.
I've served kinship and love between me and a twat.

میانِ خُود وَ جنسِ مؤنثی خویش وَ
عِشق را خِدمَت کَرده اَم.

Zane jadu dad,
The witch replied,

زَنِ جادو پاسُخ داد،

Shashe Parvin kasif
ast. Shashe Hasan kasif ast.
Inja darmane ehteyajatan ast.
Beman dah barat ra bedehid
va veda' beknoid.
Parvin's piss is dirty. Hasan's piss is dirty. Here's the curse you
want. Give me ten dollars and leave.

شاشِ پَروین کثیف است. شاشِ حَسَن
کثیف است. اینجا دَرمانِ احتیاجِتان است.
بِمَن دَه بَراترا بِدهید وَ وِداع بِکُنید.

'Ali be u dah baratra dad va
veda' kard.
Ali gave her ten dollars and left.

عَلی بِه او دَه بَراترا داد وَ وِداع کَرد.

(THE STAGE IS LEFT WITH THE CRIES OF PEACOCKS.)

END

103

TRANSLATIONS OF THE DIARIES
OF
LAURE THE SCHOOLGIRL

NO FORM
CAUSE I DON'T GIVE A SHIT
ABOUT ANYTHING ANYMORE

This writing is all just fake (copied from other writing)
so you should go away and not read any of it.

①

WHAT I SEE

It is a very Parisian garden in which I'm going to hide myself. Me, the schoolgirl. Me, with my whips. Hide myself from the outside world because I've been hurt.

Behind skeletal trees of tiny leaves a man leaves, he is totally white, shakes a fist at nothing, pisses on the tiny white garden stones, oh I am lonely, again departs, precautionarily walking around this lawn...another man rises, totally red-faced, his lips are rosy and soft as a baby's, he had me when I was encased in prison. I am not. Thousands of fuchsias surrounded me: ivy, soot, gook made out of begonia petals by her nervous fingers because they know they're almost out-of-existence like the marks of hopscotch on a bombed-out city street. The man I know is getting near me but now there are detours, this is a miniature golf course,...and another man sticks his leg through the window, bewildered face like a lunatic's, palms vertically flat beat the air, froth comes from his mouth. "Bastards. They've stolen me."

I think to myself, "I understand what you're saying."

A woman is passing by this garden. Her hands are clasped under her chin. She is a nun. She is a penguin. They aren't women because they don't have anything between their legs. They run with bodies waddling, these Catholics, flaccid flabby and dumb. Dumb nun.

104

High-up a small sallow face sticks itself into small window bars, then sticks its back hair into small window bars. I see white arms that are as thin and even as sticks.

The arm is cut-off.

The one who sees is cut-off.

Dear Georges,

It seems that everything that happens to me is all chance.

I don't like saying anything important.

But I want to tell you, only you, that I am so desperate I no longer have any fantasies.

Of course it's not necessary to say anything to you:

(1) because you always know everything.

(2) because *you don't care at all for me* meaning I *don't care for you:* meaning: *I don't want anyone in my life.*

I can't remain this frigid.

When we first met I thought you didn't notice me because I'm invisible so I said whatever I wanted to—your saying "I'll never love you" was what I wanted cause I'd remain invisible.

This is all sentimentality. I'm just surprised that given my ridiculous sentimentality, we're friends. Sometimes I want to break off everything with you because I hate you so much because you don't give me anything I want everything is your way: you don't have money you don't have time you don't love me

I'd rather be frigid.

                                                                              Laure

a   b   c   d   e

I can no longer speak.

a   b

I'm no longer apart from the world.

a

I don't know how to count yet.

A few days later:

Dear Georges,
        If you want to keep knowing me, you can telephone me now and then,

Since I have to keep myself apart from everyone, I have to keep the control.

I'm sure you're going to get to fuck lots of women.

Is anything ever understood between people? It wasn't between me and Peter.

Please don't think I'm totally malicious especially about what a whore you are.

A side of me has sincere friendship and true solidarity.

Laure

②

I BEGIN TO FEEL

I remember the corpses stood up before me. There's a creep on T.V., asking me to call him about my grandparents, but my grandparents are dead.

The corpses say: "You were born beautiful rich and smart you little creep and beauty wealth and intelligence just brought you down to deterrence, secretion, to reject you...You came from a good family even though your real father was a murderer and your mother was crazy. Even being a creep won't save you. Tonight you're going to be ours."

They're babbling tenderly to me:

This is the corpses' song:

This is Christ the eternal humiliant, the insane tyrant. He and the corpses are holding me in their arms.

The only thing that matters to me is waking up.

I begin walking to look for that moment that will wake me up.

The only thing that is satisfactory is this moment.

Soon money isn't enough for me whether American or Arabian, I float, suspended between the sky and the earth, suspended between the sky and the earth, between floor and ceiling. My dumbly sad eyes which always see things opposite to the ways they are my dumbly sad eyes which always see things opposite to the ways they are are showing their stringy lobes to the world, my mutilated hooks reveal my mother's madness reveal my mother's madness.

My mother tells me why I was born: she had a pain in her stomach, it was during the war, she went to some quack doctor (she had just married this guy because it was the war and she loved his parents); the doctor tells her she should get pregnant to cure the pain. Since she's married, she gets pregnant, but the pain stays. She won't get an abortion because she's too scared. She runs to the toilet because she thinks she has to shit; I come out. The next day she has appendicitis.

At night in every city I live in I walk down the streets to look for something that will mean something to me.

The city I dreamt of: It was here that I heard the voice of Mary the Whore Who Gave Her All For Love, here I stared at the beautiful look of Violette injected by the blackest ink, here finally Justus and Betelgeuse, Verax and Hair and all the girls with the names of stars the openings of doors magnetized the young girls. They no longer know what they're doing. Invisible rays make this nothingness where everything is possible, possible.

Anonymity by imposing no image reveals space.

This is the beginning of love. For you it's of no importance but for me it has every importance.

You also said: "You don't understand why I'm bothering with you because I have so much to give and you have nothing to give."

I'm not bothering with you now.

I hate you you took me. "I don't understand why you're bothering with me" meant I'm *not going to give anything to you.*

I'm being a bitch now saying all this. Chauffeur. It doesn't matter where you're taking me: to the furnace, to the toilet, to the brothel you're working in, now you won't see me. The only thing I need is to burn; myself torn into pieces scattered each bit away from every other, covered in your shit; and I feel every fuck that happens, every fuck frightens me. Past your taking me.

To sleep inside your left shoulder.

My real being alive will never occur where there is rigidity of mentality—too bad for my mind.

③

THE DESPERATE NEEDS
I FEEL ARE NOW BURNING

On a beach which is burning up, I discovered the sky. Immense and cloudless sky. I saw a kite. Believing I could follow this kite if I kept my eyes on it, I kept on running. I was out of breath. I threw myself on the sand. The sands slunk between my fingers like a hot caress on my cunt lips making laughter.

The penguins dragged me back through the streets while they threw icy looks at a house of sin whose windows reflected the purple sun.

This was the first day of life, love Christ, in which I really saw.

This technique of erasure.

(from now on, disintegrate the language),

I usually spent every afternoon alone and never let anyone into my house. One afternoon, two close friends with a man I didn't know came into the house. Since the situation was unexpected and my nerves are sharp, I decided we should drink as much and take as many drugs as we could lay our hands on.

About two hours later I thought it wise to put some clothes on. Somewhere around dinner-time, G (the stranger) and I kissed. By 11:00 we couldn't keep our hands off each other.

G explained in no way would he ever- jeopardize the situation between the woman he was living with and himself. I said I didn't interfere with marriages I wasn't interested in them. Even though it was the first time, our bodies worked well together. I made sure he knew I wanted him to return to his lover.

The next day I wanted to see him again and wondered if I would.

Two days later he phoned me he had tried to phone me

no feelings involved. On the way out of the sauna he met two old tricks.

I don't remember when he phoned me again. I had bought him some opium. He came to my house to pick it up. This was so early in the morning I. When I explained to him I now felt about him, he was saying he no longer wanted to fuck me because he wanted to be friends with me. When he said this same thing a few hours later over the phone, I hung up on him.

Today I don't love you.

Sometimes I have to make up you leaving me. They are not speaking to each other. They are standing apart. G is looking at the young woman. She continues to stare at the ground. Finally he says, still with the same smile, "All right. It'll be just the way you want it."

But, after a silence and while the man bows in a respectful salute, which can only be a mockery for he loves someone else, by which he appears to be taking his leave, I suddenly raise my head and hold out one hand in the uncertain gesture of a person asking for another moment of attention, or pleading for a last reprieve, or trying to interrupt an irrevocable action already performed or trying to interrupt an irrevocable action already performed you are going to leave me, saying slowly, in a low voice: "No. Don't go...Please. .. Don't leave me right away."

Of course you leave me.

It is at this moment that my heart breaks open.

2

Here you are under all sorts of signs, mad Holiness' Not very long ago Veronique smiled at me in the greasy linen of Christ, the Virgin and her halo trembles in frankincense like her Son's hands with huge nails stuck in them and the drops of blood, Saint Face is crying oily tears behind a red lamp. The red lamp is the only illumination in THE CHAPEL OF SEVEN PAINS. It was the retreat, the hour of meditation. I am seven years old, I am seven years old. I am spitting on the blood of my dead father, suicided mother, and separated husband.

One more time Christ lodged himself in my attic.

This attic is falling-down-all-over-the-place closed by its walls to the outside and so full of bits of un- or half-recognizable materials you feel happily enclosed full of things which should travel everywhere and go nowhere and pieces of once-luxurious china now so cracked good-for-nothing. The window is always shut.

My grandmother is a member of royalty. Her hair is pale, her nose is thin, and her cheekbones are high. One day she phoned me to ask for help. When I reached her hotel room, I found her crawling across the floor. Peter took one look at her, said "Excuse men and left. My sister, the good member of the family, refused to help her so I, the bad member, was the only one who cared for her in the hospital. The hospital sensory intellectual and dietetic deprivation gave her a kidney infection, then senility. She said, "I'm going blind" and the doctors said, "She's not going blind." The kidney infection was under control so I went to Europe as I had planned to. I wrote her every other day. In Paris, when my master gave me his apartment, for the first time I was alone, for no reason for the first time I phoned my grandmother. She asked me to come home. I didn't understand her words. The nurse said she would phone me back. Two hours later, the nurse said I had phoned my grandmother in the last hour I had been able to.

I would remain here for hours, escaping the horrible outside world, plunging through mine to the non-material. One day the jumble of hodgepodge and rat-trap bits was gone. I reached the one window and opened it. This was the only place where you could see a balloon fallen into a neighboring garden. It was twenty feet from a boat held between two walls. The orange plastic, as the air slowly leaks out of it, snakes, no longer bound in strings, slithers across the roofs and branches. Finally it is disentangling itself from the jumble of THINGS:

What my mother says is true: I am born out of and by nothing.

This little shit by being insolent and deceptive is making its way toward freedom.

I am what wakes me up.

I'm being woken up when I'm feeling a combination of fear and pleasure.

This combination is called CURIOSITY.

What makes me feel fear?
    MAID: Why do you keep me?
    HAMM: There's no one else.
    MAID: There's nowhere else.
        (pause.)
    HAMM: You're leaving me all the same.
    MAID: I'm trying.
    HAMM: You don't love me.
    MAID: Once!
    HAMM:I've made you suffer too much.

110

        (pause.)
        Haven't I?
MAID: It's not that.
HAMM (shocked): I haven't made you suffer too much?
MAID: Yes!
HAMM: (relieved): Ah you gave me a fright!
        (pause. coldly.)
        Forgive me.
        (pause. louder.)
        I said, Forgive me.
MAID: I heard you.
        (pause.)
        Have you bled?
HAMM: Less.
        (pause.)
        Isn't it time for my pain-killer?
MAID: No.
        (pause.)
HAMM: How are your eyes?
MAID: Bad.
HAMM: How are your legs?
MAID: Bad.
HAMM: But you can move.
MAID: Yes.
HAMM (violently): Then move!
        (The maid goes to the back wall, leans against it with
        her forehead and hands.)
        Where are you?
MAID: Here.
HAMM: Come back!
        (The maid returns to her place beside the chair.)
        Where are you?
MAID: Here.
HAMM: Why don't you kill me?
MAID: I don't know the combination of the cupboard.

GOING AGAINST THE WORLD

1

Christine, the maid's daughter, was simple and sweet. One night
her mother didn't come home at the expected time. She went to
look for her. At the police-station the police told her, "Your moth-
ers a thief and we're going to put her in prison." Christine

returned home. She sat alone all night in her room. At 6:00 A.M., no one appearing no one in her life, she threw herself out the window.

I'm not going to throw myself out the window for you though I prefer cutting my wrists.

I asked my mother why she should do such a ridiculous thing. "Don't talk about disgusting things at the dinner table, Laure." We got a new maid. I want to know reality. My mother kept screaming to me it was all the maid service's fault, the most disgusting act in the world is suicide. This is how I came to love suicide.

2

I decided to take G away for two days so I could spend my first night with him. We had dinner together the night before he kept talking about what he did with his girlfriend. I said to myself, "What do I keep paying for this guy for when he keeps talking about his girlfriend?" The next morning in the car and I AM NEVER awake in the mornings I said, "I love you and you don't love me." He said, "If you want a boyfriend I'm not it." I said, "OK. That's that." He said, "Maybe I shouldn't come this week-end." I said, "Yes." He said, "Can I call you when you get back?" I said, "No." The other guy got out of the car. We started to make out. I will fuck you anytime anywhere. He said, "I don't want you to keep me." I said, "I don't support any man." I had made up this whole incident so I could do what I wanted: fuck up the one thing that matters to me in my life.

If only someone loved me...I'd do anything to love with someone with no one...I bought a dog and cut open my stomach with a knife...I've lost control again...I see this white curly fur like it has babies inside it I want your baby and something in me turns over and dies. At eight years old I'm no longer a human being.

Now I have to stop lying:

Mommy says over and over again I don't love her.

I have decided she's right. I don't love her.

"When I think of all I've done for you and now, look at how you're talking to me, you're ice-cold."

"No, not ice-cold. Just cold."

The shit hits the fan. Mommy claims her right to my being a slave to her (this is what love is).

I am never going to love.

She who opened up and mutilated her body to give me wonderful life. I gave a black laugh and replied she hadn't wanted to have me she would have had an abortion and killed me off fast if she hadn't been so scared "as for me, I don't know if I want to be alive or dead." She threw herself into the chair, screamed that I had no idea what I was saying I was crazy she was going to put me in the asylum, and fainted. A woman's tactic. I went away. I no longer felt. I said the truth. "As for me, I don't know if I want to be alive or dead."

So being without love, am I no longer going to live?

For one time, all became as clear and transparent as blazing noon. In the blazing noon of the full of this summer I went to the garden: white butterflies flew above the canal bank, a swarm of mosquitoes came into my face, so much disappeared that now things were simple, I remained for a long time by this water edge and I saw this life is as I imagine it. There's nothing more to trespass. ■

ALGERIA
A SERIES OF INVOCATIONS
BECAUSE NOTHING ELSE WORKS

THE LAND IN ALGERIA IS PINK
LIFE IN THIS AMERICA STINKS

CUNT

IN 1979, RIGHT BEFORE THE ALGERIAN REVOLUTION
BEGINS, THE CITY IS COLD AND DANK...

①
THE STUD ENEMY

I am fucking you and you are coming you have a hard time coming you breathe hard you have periods when you strain to come then your cock withers you strain to come again. I hear you I see you I don't feel I am doing anything to help you the rhythm is so steady I come jagged to your steady rhythm my coming is insignificant compared to your building. You gasp. You are three laps away. Oh I am coming again. My coming is always so unexpected. I want you to come. I want you to come. I want you. I want you. When you come I never come you are unable to move it is always so unexpected.

I leave Kader because I live in New York City and Kader lives in Toronto. In New York I feel I'm a jagged part skin walking down the street. I feel part of my being no longer is. That is disgusting. That is an outrage.

I have to leave the man I love because I have no money and he has no money. I want to bust up the government to destroy every government that's telling me what to do, controlling the me that I most want to be me, bust up the society that causes government, the money that denies feeling and irrationality I hate

Separation from Kader makes me have to fill that separation with nothing, makes me grab at everyone, makes me hate everyone for me every single thing is equal to every other single thing: I have to get to you. I have to get to you.

114

I HATE equals I LOVE YOU.

Here in New York, every morning I wake up, I don't want to be awake. I have to persuade myself to wake up. I have to use my will to get food in my mouth because my heart sees no reason for anything. I don't feel unhappy. I don't think my life's repulsive even though I have no money for food I have to beg friends for food. I don't care about poverty. I want.

Kader and I write each other a lot. I write Kader I'm a terrorist which is obviously a lie. Kader writes me he's waiting on a subway platform when the subway comes he doesn't know whether to throw himself under it or walk into it when he gets home he sticks a knife into his own hand beats his head against the wall. I write we're not going to see each other again because we live in separate cities and we have no hope of attaining money. Kader writes me if he doesn't see me soon he'll go crazy.

The Algerian revolution began on May 8, 1945, in Setif, a largely Muslim town 80 miles west of Constantine. The town inhabitants were preparing to celebrate the Nazi capitulation to Western European forces of the previous night. The Algerians had always passively resented their French occupants. The newly formed nationalist movement Parti du Peuple Algerien (P.P.A.) was the first occasion for direct Algerian anger. Right before the anti-Nazi celebration, the French sent the leader of the P.P.A, Messali Hadj, to jail. The Muslim population of Setif wanted the anti-Nazi celebration to become a strong suggestion that the French leave Algeria to the Algerians.

Actually there was no such important rational plan. All people are hungry, wanting. Hungry people do not act by rational plans, but by instinct. During the anti-Nazi celebration, a French policeman saw a beautiful Algerian boy, got a hard-on, couldn't tell what he should do. The Algerians were carrying their green and-white national flag and banners saying "Long Live Messali" "Free Messali" "For The Liberation Of The People, Long Live Free And Independent Algeria!" Instead of fucking him up the ass, the cop shot the beautiful Algerian boy in the stomach. People act in accordance with the energy levels of their situations. The Muslims jumped the Europeans. Anger was out on the streets.

The next week the Europeans murdered 45,000 Muslims.

Over the phone I tell Kader to come to New York. He phones me he's planning to come he doesn't have any money he needs to find free rides each way and some free money. We're both feeling desperate.

Kader says he'll come to New York he'll borrow the money. I tell him if he can't get hold of the money, he's not old enough to have me. I'm forgetting who Kader is. My forgetting gets me scared cause I'm desperate to have someone else in my life.

I decide as if the decision is no part of me I stick with Kader. I ask him when are you coming to New York? Kader says he'll be here in three days because he's been able to borrow the money. I love him. I don't want him to come here, break into my isolation. My body desperately wants a cock inside her.

Before and after Setif, the French colonists were controlling more and more of Algeria and decimating more and more Algerians. By 1954 an average European in Algeria owned ten times the land an average Algerian owned and earned 25 times as much moola. The French pumped the Algerians full of penicillin and other antibiotics so the Algerians would have more kids. All these kids had no way to eat so they'd do anything for money. They were dispossessed de-everything-ed. The French Arab Culture ministers told the Arabs they'd have to stop speaking and writing their language, Arabic. They told the Arab women their Arab men had made them into slaves.

Over half-a-million Algerian Muslims a year fled to France to the garbaged cities in which they worked for French bosses for almost nothing though to them it was a lot because in Algeria the average Muslim worker earned twenty-two cents a day if he was lucky one-ninth of the population was unemployed and earned nothing.

I, Omar, live alone in a room. I almost never leave my room. I am lonely out of my mind sometimes. A lot of this time I worry a lot about money because for the last three months I have owned about ten dollars a week I am two months behind on rent I hate all other people; I am unable to fuck I am horny; I see nobody I am scared I am in danger kill kill; I am unable to kill my grandmother who is rich many people kill many people in wars I hate myself because I do not kill; because I do not walk out of my room.

Whenever a cock enters me every night three nights in a row, I ask myself regardless of who the cock belongs to should I let my SELF depend on this person or should I remain a closed entity. I say: I'm beginning to love you I don't want to see you again. The man thinks I'm crazy so he wants nothing to do with me.

The French police fastened the gégène's (an army signals magneto) electrodes to the Algerian rebel's ears and fingers. A flash of lightning exploded next to the man's ears he felt his heart racing in his breast The cops turned up the electricity. Instead of those sharp and rapid spasms, the Algerian felt more pain, convulsed muscles, longer spasms. The cop placed the electrodes in his mouth. The currents plastered his jaws against the electrodes. Images of fire luminous geometric nightmares burned across his glued eyelids. While the Algerian longed for water, they dumped his head into a bucket of ice-cold liquid until he had to breathe the liquid. They did this again and again. They did this again and again. A fist big as an ox's ball slammed into his head. The screams of other prisoners were all around him. He no longer knew he was in pain, pain was wrong, living wasn't a constant fire of torture and disgust. The moment before the Algerian went crazy and accepted horror as usual, his greatest fear and torment was this consciousness that he, the Algerian, is about to go crazy, has to give up his mind which is anger and accept the horrible inequality, the French way of living he is fighting against

THE PROBLEM OF WE THE COLONIZED

All those people of whom we are afraid, who crush the jealous emerald of our dreams, who twist the fragile curve of our smiles, all those people we face, who ask us no questions, but to whom we put strange ones:

Who are they?

What can our enthusiasm and devotion and madness achieve if everyday reality is now a tissue of lies, a tissue of cowardice, a tissue of contempt for human mentality?

The degree of alienation of the people who gave me this world seems frightening to me. Alien to alienation, we now have to live depersonalized or....

Right now there is no difference between a legal and a criminal act. Lawlessness, inequality for the sake of desire, multi-daily murders of human beings have been raised to the status of legislated middle-class principles.

This social structure negates our beings, makes us who are without into nothings. If we hope: if we talk of or search for love,

this hope is not an open door to the future, but the illogical main-
tenance of a subjective attitude in organized contradiction with
reality.

Beneath the lousy material way we live, beneath our petty
crimes, we want to eat food without roach-eggs and we want to
love people. I think a society that drives its members to desperate
solutions is a non-viable society, a society to be replaced.

HOW CAN I WHO AM DISINHERITED ACT?

I have to make Kader here even if he isn't here. I talk to
Kader on the streets. I write down the conversations I have with
Kader over the phone. I use Kader for everything. I can't write
down what I think I should be writing Kader's thoughts keep
interrupting me. I have to fuck I have to fuck I have to fuck I

I think that for a kid American family life is so bad (cause the
parents, taking shit from their parents, bosses, the media, etc.,
have only their kid to dump on), that all a kid can do these days
by the time he has his first chance to try to control a little of his
life is find some decent parents so maybe he can grow up. Each
young person is desperately trying to find a parent. Since there
are no adults now, there are no other relationships.

Kader is in New York now. I don't feel anything for him.

After the French murdered 45,000 Muslims, they seized and
imprisoned the rest of the rebel leaders. But the Algerian people
didn't stop being angry. The young Algerian boys who were
growing up knew smatterings of Marxist revolutionary tech-
niques. They didn't care for liberal sentiments or revolutionary
discussions. They weren't interested in groups. They enjoyed
hating. They liked to fight. They respected violence.

②
CUNT

All Algerian women wear the veil. This large square cloth
that covers the whole face and body makes the woman anonymous. There is no such thing as a woman. Henceforth a woman is
A CUNT. A CUNT can see. It cannot be seen. A CUNT does not
yield itself it does not offer itself it does not give itself. The
Frenchmen who say they want cunt find real CUNTS frustrating.

This is the way THE CUNT my mother committed suicide:
THE CUNT ate at the most expensive restaurants in New

York City. It purchased five copies of every expensive piece of clothing it liked. It bought needlepoint designs at $300 a piece. It rode in taxis and hired limousines. THE CUNT ran through $300,000 of its husband's life insurance money and the money THE CUNT its mother gave it in two years. The closer THE CUNT came to no money, the more frenzily it spent. It stole money and jewelry from THE CUNT its mother. It ran out of jewelry it could steal from THE CUNT its mother. So it began to buy $50 a piece hangars and $20 a pair socks from Bloomingdales so it could spend more and more money.

THE CUNT was the one who came the closest to successful suicide by blowing money.

THE CUNT was left with no money and no source of money. Its apartment in which it had lived for thirty years was about to be taken away from it because it hadn't paid rent in three months. Since its friends were close to a CUNT who had lots of money like them, it was about to have no friends. It had never worked for money. It had no idea how to live in this world.

Its empty hole was arising.

THE CUNT'S THE CUNT mother had made two million by marrying a rich man when it was thirty years old. On Monday THE CUNT asked THE CUNT its mother for money. THE CUNT mother refused. Now THE CUNT had driven itself as close to suicide by money as it could get. Money is simply rejection.

THE ACTUAL SUICIDE:

On Thursday, THE CUNT dressed itself in its new navy blue suit THE CUNT packed another suit, a skirt, a sweater, a pair of black patent leather shoes, a nightie, a bathrobe, two pairs of nylon underpants, a pair of sheer panty hose, a bra, and a small overnight case containing cigarettes, reading glasses, a red lipstick, bobby pins, and three bottles of the diet pills and Librium THE CUNT had been eating since its dead husband's first heart attack eight years ago in a large cloth green-and-black plaid valise. THE CUNT opened the gray metal safety vault stored under the shoe shelf. It put all the papers except for bills, my adoption papers, and its medical insurance back in the vault

THE CUNT transported the valise, the vault, and its brown poodle Mistaflur to the New York Hilton Hotel. When the New York Hilton hotel refused to accept its expired Master Charge card, THE CUNT slipped them a bad check. THE CUNT told the New York Hilton Hotel it wasn't sure how many nights it planned to stay there; it would pay in advance for two nights. At noon

THE CUNT walked the half block to THE CUNT its mother's hotel. It balanced THE CUNT its mother's bankbooks. THE CUNT was speedier and more agitated than usual.

The next day THE CUNT boarded its poodle at Dr. Wolborn's on 51st street off Third Avenue. THE CUNT told THE CUNT receptionist it'd pick up Mistaflur on the Tuesday after the upcoming Christmas.

THE CUNT had no one no thing. THE CUNT had no more time no more space. But THE CUNT had itself. In the hotel room THE CUNT ate down all its Librium and died.

SUICIDE AND SELF-DESTRUCTION
IS THE FIRST WAY THE SHITTED-ON START SHOWING
ANGER AGAINST THE SHITTERS.

③
THE NEXT CRAZY CUNT

Name:	OMAR
Education:	Up to two years graduate school
Occupation:	Nothing
Former Convictions:	1971-Obscenity lowered to Contempt, $50. fine. Twice.

THE CUNTS are heard, dense like the cries of birds, shrill, metallic, angry.

Today I go to visit THE CUNT my grandmother. THE CUNT my grandmother is very rich and I am very poor. My husband who left me eight months ago met me on the streetcorner. He was fifteen minutes late. I was very upset at him because if we're not on time THE CUNT my grandmother who is a dictator throws a fit On the street I threw my husband's mail at him.

In retaliation he told me no one treats him with as little respect as I treat him. He had ACTUALLY been looking forward to seeing me, but now he didn't want to go with me to THE CUNT my grandmother's. I was not the person I now was. I have no pride in myself. To survive I must learn how to do things for money.

In my mind I don't want to see my husband again because I don't like him. But THE CUNT my grandmother likes me only when I'm married so I have to keep pretending I'm married. I

HAVE to. Since it knows Ali and I are married, I have to keep pretending I'm married to Ali.

The moment we walk into THE CUNT my grandmother's apartment, it asks me why I'm neglecting it. It would have left its apartment if it could walk. I apologize as abjectly as I know how. Ali laughs.

THE CUNT my grandmother's CUNT companion enters. THE CUNT my grandmother wants to eat in The Museum of Modern Art around the corner. Since it can't walk anymore, it and its companion take a taxi around the block. Ali and I are supposed to walk.

Ali and I are waiting an hour on The Museum of Modern Art lunch line. THE CUNT companion is escorting THE CUNT my grandmother to a table in the garden. A sign above the tables says NO RESERVING. THE CUNT my grandmother holding on to THE CUNT its companion for dear life stands right over THE CUNTS sitting at its favorite table until those CUNTS leave. Then THE CUNT my grandmother sits itself down and waits.

As soon as Ali and I reach the food counter, THE CUNT companion walks THE CUNT my grandmother over to our place in the line so THE CUNT my grandmother can pick its own food. It doesn't trust anybody. THE CUNT its companion walks it back to the table so the table doesn't get lost, walks back to the food counter, pays for all our food, walks back and forth to carry all the food to the table. THE CUNT my grandmother doesn't allow us to do anything. Then, from its very own plate, THE CUNT my grandmother gives one lettuce leaf, one peach slice, and a spoonful of egg salad smothered in pink French dressing to THE CUNT its companion.

THE CUNT my grandmother keeps ordering THE CUNT its companion to fetch us different silverware and drinks. Ali keeps disappearing into a phone booth to try to get away from here as soon as possible. THE CUNT my grandmother is keeping to its two topics of conversation: food and THE dead CUNT my mother. Why don't you eat more, Omar? Eat this piece of cheesecake. Eat this apple pie. I slip the food to Ali so I don't vomit. Why does Ali eat so much? With what food costs these days, it's ridiculous to waste food. Wrap this leftover vomit in a napkin and put it in your bag. If you don't take the vomit, THE CUNT companion will. THE CUNT companion is such a pig, she'll take any vomit. THE CUNT your mother wasn't a pig: it was perfect. It was absolutely beautiful. Everyone loved it. Why'd it have to kill itself. You'd be exactly like it, Omar, if only you'd grow your hair and act feminine.

I ask THE CUNT my grandmother about the places it's travelled to. Ali and I escort THE CUNT my grandmother with great dignity to a taxi-cab and we take a subway home.

I have to sell two gold watches: all THE CUNT my mother left me. I'm walking in the Diamond district. Ali yells at me I'll want these watches as mementoes. I yell I want to pay my rent, Con Ed, and tax return bills I'm two months late on. The gold dealer is a shifty cold man. He tells me my watches aren't real gold.

④

OMAR MEETS A REBEL

THE BATTLE OF ALGIERS

5 p.m. The street is fairly wide for a street in the Arab quarter. By this late afternoon it is crowded with Algerians in traditional clothes and Europeans dressed as Europeans

NOBODY. I AM NOBODY. I LIVE ON ILLEGAL UNEMPLOYMENT AND SHIT JOBS. I AM TOO OLD TO BE ATTRACTIVE. AT NIGHT I WALK THE STREETS FOR ENJOYMENT. I AM ADJUSTING TO LIFE.

Omar: This is an Arab cafe on Rue Random 40. Its owner, Madjebri, is a police informer. . .

THE CUNT DIGS UP **THE CUNT** ITS DEAD MOTHER; RIPS OFF ITS GOLD JEWELRY AND THE GOLD FILLINGS IN ITS TEETH.

Omar: Everyday at 5 p.m. a French cop walks into the cafe supposedly for a cup of tea. Medjebri tells him what's happening in the quarter.

Medjebri moves away from his register to the table the cop's sitting at. He mutters hello and hands the cop a cup of tea.
    The cop sips his cup of tea It's so hot he has to drink slowly. Finally he finishes. Medjebri walks to the table, picks up the cup and mutters some words. He walks away with the cup.

*A large clock and sign for vacuum cleaners. Under
the clock and sign for vacuum cleaners a young CUNT
stands motionless. Its arms, forming an arch, balance a
basket on its head.*

*The cop hands Medjebri some money for his tea
Medjebri refuses.*

*Omar is standing under the clock and sign. He and
THE CUNT exchange glances.*

*THE CUNT shifts the basket filled with corn on to
its hip.*

It and Omar walk toward the cafe.

*The cop walks out of the cafe. He shoves his way
through the Algerians who want to get into the cafe.*

He walks down the street.

*Omar and THE CUNT are following the cop. They
have a hard time winding through the crowds of people
so they keep the correct distance behind the cop.*

*THE CUNT sticks its hand into the corn. It hands
Omar a small revolver.*

*Omar keeps the revolver under his jacket. He tries
to pass the cop.*

THE CUNT holds him back. It's scared.

He smiles at it. His eyes glint.

*He moves a few steps past the policeman.
Suddenly he turns, lifts his arm as if to hit him, extends
the revolver. The cop halts. His eyes wide. Instinctively
he raises his hands. He's terrified out of his mind.*

*Omar looks around him. People are running away
from him. Others are mesmerized and can't run.*

Omar: Don't move. Look you. Look at him! He doesn't give orders
now. His hands are up. Do you see him, brothers? The people
who control us are just like us.

*Omar presses the trigger. An empty click. Omar
presses the trigger several times.*

The gun barrel is empty.

*The cop lowers his right hand. It almost touches his
gun.*

*Omar throws away his gun and jumps. He knocks
down the surprised cop.*

*The crowd spread. Omar starts to punch out the
cop and stops. He thinks of THE CUNT who handed him*

123

the empty gun. THE CUNT is stashing the rod in her corn and running.

Omar hits at the cop, gets up, runs after THE CUNT.

When he reaches her, he grabs her shoulders so roughly, he's about to beat on her, but COP WHISTLES, the cops are almost up to them, so they run away together.

They reach an alleyway. As Omar is about to get THE CUNT it enters a front door.

THE CUNT places the basket on the floor, removes the gun and hides the gun next to its tits. As it turns, Omar blocks its way.

Omar: Tell me what's going on here. Who sent me that letter?

CUNT: If we don't get out of here now, they'll catch us.

Omar: (*uncontrollably*): I want to know.

⑤
MADNESS BEGINS

:KNOCK. KNOCK. KNOCK.

Omar is looking at his white door.

Omar: Who is it?

:The most important person in your life.

Omar opens his door. His landlord is standing in the hall way.

Omar (*quickly*): Here's the rest of your money. (*Hands the French Landlord an envelope.*)

French Landlord: What're you paying now?

Omar: $160

French landlord: You're lucky.

Omar: I'm lucky?

French Landlord: I'm getting $225 for these apartments now.

Omar: You can't get $225 from me. It's the law. You can only raise me seven and a half percent.

French Landlord: I'm just joking, I'm just jokeeng. I wouldn't say this if it wasn't a joke. I wouldn't say it if it wasn't t a joke. Let's see...71/2% raise means you owe me (*they figure out Omar's new rent*). You know last month I was ready to break into this apartment and give it to someone else.

Omar: You've got your rent. O.K? Goodbye.

PHOEBES, a restaurant on the Bowery. A group of six poor musicians and artists are sitting at one of the tables in the front behind the large glass windows which serve as walls. A famous rock-n-roll star walks into the restaurant and asks if he can sit with these people.

CUNT: You're Mick Jagger, aren't you? Oooo. Can I have your autograph?

He signs its tit and it walks away.

Mick Jagger: I can't really deal with being this famous.

CUNT Waitress: Would you like anything to eat?

Mick Jagger: An omelette and some french fries, and a glass of white wine.

Various CUNTS keep running up to Mick Jagger and getting his autograph. The musicians and artists talk among themselves. Mick Jagger pulls out a wad of hundred dollar bills to pay for his food

Mick Jagger to CUNT Waitress: I 'm sorry. This is the only money I've got.

CUNT: You shouldn't carry that kind of money around in this neighborhood. It's dangerous.

Mick Jagger: It's not that much money. It's just the pocket change I keep on me.

AREAS OF THE CASBAH UNDERWORLD. VOODOO. CHICKEN AND ONE-LEGGED BEGGARS DANCE IN THE AIR. THE POOR PEOPLE ARE SMIRKING EVERY-WHERE.

At the bottom of the Casbah is this whore section. Black bars for gamblers and opium smokers.

People who can no longer manage: Dirty old men Children. CUNTS. The old men lie on the streets. Rub their cocks. The children deal drugs and dirty pictures. CUNTS, if they're young, are standing by their door-ways, looking for Johns. They've tied their veils, away from their faces, over their heads, at their neck napes.

Omar is walking down the Street of The Reflection of Stars. Only a few windows in the Casbah show lights. Night. In the background there is the triumphant neon of the European city: the sea, the ships at rest, that lighthouse beams. Omar wants. Worse than wanting and not getting is feeling that now he's used to—I don't have to repeat again the material evidences of depriva-tion: living in garbage, no food, disease, lousy sexual relations, poisoned air, no control—being a robot; accepting that he's living a half-life a sedated life a machine life soon he'll not even be conscious that there's another way to live than the way he's dying. He has to fight. He has to find. He SCREAMS. The depres-sion comes down more and more. Omar can't move. He stops walking through the streets. Depression is a cold heavy weight on top of him. Is him. He cannot move.

Rue de Thebes. An automobile slows down at the first stop sign. A man sticks his head out the window and looks.

The Car Driver: Right or left?   (*These are heard as whispers in the night*)

The Man Whose Head Is Out: Try going to the right.

The car turns right. Moves slowly down the street. The numbers, even, are growing. 26. . . 28. . . 30. . .

The Car Driver: What's the number?

The Man Whose Head Was Out: 8.

A Man Sitting In The Back Of The Car: It doesn't matter. Stop here.

The Man Whose Head Was Out: It does matter. Back up until you're directly opposite 8.

In the shadows Omar is watching.

A streetlight hits the car at an angle so we see the men inside the car are French cops.

The car backs up past the stop sign, 16... 14... 12... 10..., to 8. The Car Driver, the French Police Commissioner, puts the car in neutral. His right hand is pressing in the cigarette lighter in the dashboard.

The Man Who Leaned His Head Out Of The Window, the French Assistant Police Commissioner, picks up a large package lying under his legs. Its wrapping is large pieces of newspaper. He gives it to the cop sitting in the back seat. The cop leans it against the back seat, gently feels around in the newspapers until he finds the right spot, removes the newspaper from that part and pulls out a small plastic tube.

The Assistant Police Commissioner: How long are you giving us?

Cop: Five minutes. Give me a light.

The Police Commissioner pulls the cigarette lighter out of the dashboard. Meanwhile the Cop has opened the back car door. Very quickly: he takes the lighter and touches the fuse. Sparks.

#8 door is directly opposite the open car door.

The Cop places the package in a shadow under #8 door while the Police Commissioner changes gears.

The Cop races back to the car.

At the second he is jumping into the car, the Police Commissioner is releasing the clutch. The police car shoots away.

The explosion is very violent. The building fronts #8, #10 and

#12 burst and collapse.

The explosion echoes end. There's a long no-sound. Within: a few sharp recognizable lonely noises: Bricks fall. Glass shatters...

Omar walks into the rubble as the clear white light of dawn appears. This light is dispelling every shadow and precisely designing every outline. Omar can see clearly. Here and there, in the middle of the sky, numerous dust clouds appear, strangely motionless. Omar sees a few human figures. They look black. They scuttle like ants across the debris. CUNTS, motionless, weep softly. Their moans are so low they sound like prayers. Here and there: a scream, a sob, a sound of running.

The black figures pull human limbs and bodies out of the rubble.

There is no pity in the lower streets and alleys of the Casbah. There is hatred and anger.

People run and shout through the streets. They lean out their windows or stand on their balconies and scream.

Ju-Ju Ju-Ju Ju-Ju Ju-Ju Ju-Ju Ju-Ju Ju-Ju Ju-Ju Ju-Ju Ju-Ju Ju-Ju
Ju-Ju Ju-Ju Ju-Ju Ju-Ju Ju-Ju Ju-Ju Ju-Ju Ju-Ju Ju-Ju Ju-Ju Ju-Ju

These Ju-Jus smother every other sound. The excitement is increasing. The people are running to where there is more running, a louder shouting. They don't know what they want to do except they want to be together. A man points downward: to the clean houses of the French.

The European Quarter

The top of steep, almost vertical steps that lead from the Casbah to the European quarter.

Dusk. In the European city the first fake lights are visible. Europeans begin to crowd the bars for an aperitif.

A bar on Rue Marengo.

BLACK ORPHEUS

The room isn't large enough to be an auditorium, but it is an auditorium. It's back rank as I see it in my dream, which is the first place Omar stands: THE PLACE FOR SPECTATORS, lies above the rest of the room. Its walls and ceiling are black. There's a feeling of red. A waist-high black metal bar separates THE PLACE FOR SPEC-TATORS from the rest of the auditorium.

The black metal bar three feet from each end of the room, in turning downward, forms two movie-house-like aisles on each side of the auditorium. These aisles are descending ramps. Covered with red velvet. This may or may not be.

The center part of the auditorium is very large. People are standing in a slipshod circle at the edges of this part.

These people wear clean white. Three men in the center front of the room play drums. Huge black velvet curtains sweep over them and almost hide them. A thin man who doesn't wear white with an American Indian headdress and a cigar in his mouth walks right up to the drummers, looks at them, flicks his cigar in their faces, turns around looks at the people in the circle, puts the cigar in his mouth, walks away. As he walks away, he nods his approval. All these gestures are precise. The people start to move.

Omar is standing in the right part of THE PLACE FOR SPECTATORS. He is alone. He is looking down into the room below. •

Man With Headdress: You won't find her that way.

Omar looks up at the Man With Headdress.

Man With Headdress: If you really want to find Eurydice, you'll have to join us.

The Man With Headdress walks down a flight of black stairs to the center room. He unbuckles the red velvet restaurant-like rope that separates the bottom of the stairs from the rest of the lower room, ushers Omar through, and rebuckles the belt.

The Man With Headdress blows cigar smoke in Omar's face. The central room. A short fat CUNT enters the middle of this room. It should be middle-aged, but it's wearing a very short clean white ruffled baby dress tied around the waist by a thin light blue satin ribbon. Another pale satin ribbon tied around its hair. It begins to slowly turn. It hiccups. As soon as it hiccups, its character changes. It dominates the room. It's the greatest dancer in the world. It smokes a cigar. It becomes a dominant male. He knows what's going on. He stamps. More and more people turn. The circle's borders slowly become less defined The Man With Headdress directs the thickening traffic.

Omar is walking through these dancers because he's obsessively searching.

During this scene the following song is chanted in the background,

:Prié pou' tou les morts:
pou' les morts 'bandonné nan gran bois,
pou' les morts 'bandonné nan gran dlo,
pou' les morts 'bandonné nan gran plaine,
pou' les morts tué pa' couteau,
pou' les morts tué pa' épée,
pou' tou les morts, au nom de Mait' Cafou et de Legba;
pou' tou generation paternelle et maternelle,
ancêtre et ancetère, Afrique et Afrique;
au nom de Mait' Cafou, Legba, Baltaza, Miroi. . .

Pray for the dead you undecided:
for the dead roaming in the great wood,
for the dead roaming in the great sea,
for the dead roaming in the great waste,
for you killed by knives,
for you killed violently,
for you dead, in the name of Legba, Master of Decide,
for my mother's and father's generation who accepted slavery,

in the name of Legba, No-Slave, Master of Decide, the Mirror:

pray

The Man With Headdress walks up to Omar.

Man With Headdress: It's over. You can go now.

Omar Where's Eurydice?

Man With Headdress: It'll be following you.

Omar, (*clutching the Man With Headdress' arm*): I don't see it.
I want...

*All the dancers laugh. They think Omar's crazy cause he
isn't happy and that's funny.*

Omar, (*more confused*): Where's Eurydice?

Man With Headdress: If you don't trust us, you'll never get it. You
have to trust it's behind you.

Omar I want to see it! Once!

*Omar is looking behind him. He's seeing the short fat
CUNT who started the dancing following him. He's
thinking it's ugly.*

Omar: That's not Eurydice!

CUNT Eurydice: Omar...Omar...(*The short fat CUNT's voice tells
us it's Eurydice. Its arms reach out to Omar, but it can no longer
follow him.*)

Man With Headdress to Omar You have to get out of here now.

Omar is in a stupor. He's leaving.

THE ABOVE IS AN INVOCATION
SO I CAN TRY TO GET LOVE BACK

Levi-Strauss: Meaning depends on rules. Is rules. That's the
nature of language.

5 p.m. A stage in the upstairs of FUN CITY on 42nd street. The downstairs of FUN CITY is filled with dirty movie booths. In front of the stage are twelve rows of stained red plush chairs
The fake red velvet stage curtains are open. A huge bed covered by a filthy dazzling pink terrycloth throw is center stage. To the left of this bed, a broken armchair. The light is pink. The joint smells of dried piss and come. Omar, a young boy-CUNT, and Hacene, a tall lean stud who never fucks CUNTS, are on stage.

CUNT, (*running on to the stage*): You've been discovered! You've been discovered!

Omar, (*jumping like an excited dog over Hacene*): We're discovered! We're in! Hacene! Hacene! (*Turning to* THE CUNT,) John Belushi was here last night

CUNT: You're going to be a big movie star.

OMAR: I'm famous. I'll have rows and rows of satin shoes. I'll fuck! I'll be (*wiggling her hips slightly*) who I am. I AM Omar.

Hacene: I'm going to buy that gorgeous new Bill Blass suit and that set of champagne glasses Mourad saw yesterday.

Omar: The world's wonderful!...(*Jumps up and down on the broken-glass-covered bed*) I'm not going to be miserable anymore! I'm not poor! I'm going to see doctors for the next two weeks! I'm going to travel wherever I want to go!

Hacene: Calm down, honey. 5:30. We've got a show to do.(*Hacene and Omar somewhat control the shows because FUN CITY's boss, a Mafiosa, never walks upstairs cause he's scared of getting busted.*)

Omar: Doing a sex show's great! Now that we've been discovered. The only thing I mind is being busted.

Hacene: What show do you want to do? (*He and Omar have a repertory of three semi-improvised shows they keep rotating so they don't become bored out of their minds.)*

> *Hacene's slowly closing the stage curtains.*

Omar: I don't want to get busted again. Let's do the psychiatrist one. This time let's play the audience hard: I'll really google at them when I tell you how men are always watching me.

Hacene: I'll say you're really stupid. I'll heap insults on you.

Omar: I'll act as dumb as I know.

> *The stage curtains open up. Half-way the right curtain sticks; Hacene runs on stage and pulls it open.*
> *Hacene's sitting in the armchair to the right of the huge bed. He's wearing a dark suit that's seen better days. Omar enters STAGE RIGHT. It's wearing its version (as close as it can stand to be) of an uptown CUNT's shopping outfit. It walks past Hacene and turns around to face him:*

Omar: Oh doctor. I hope I'm not early. I hope it's O.K.

Hacene in a smooth voice: It's fine, Mrs. er...(*Looks down at a slip of paper.*) Or is it Miss?

Omar: Miss.

Hacene: I'll make a note to remind my receptionist. Just sit down, Miss Fendermast (*getting its name right*) and relax yourself.

Omar: Uh...(*looking around. It can't find where to sit.*)

Hacene: Just sit down here, Miss Fendermast. I'm sure you'll feel comfortable.

Omar (*jumping away like it SEES it for the first time*): That's a bed!

Hacene: Yes, Miss Fendermast. I find it helps create the proper atmosphere in which my patient can feel free to express himself to the fullest extent possible.

Omar: I can't sit on a BED!

Hacene: Miss Fendermast, are you scared of beds? Really now. It won't bite you. Try sitting on the bed. If you don't like it, you can talk standing up.

Omar: I'll talk standing up.

Hacene: Well, Miss Fendermast, (*shifting in his seat*), what seems to be the problem?

Omar (*nervously agitating, blocking*): I don't know, doctor. I don't think there is any problem. I don't know why I came here.

Hacene: Why don't you just talk, Miss Fendermast? Tell me something about yourself.

Omar: There's nothing to tell. . . I'm not anybody. . .

Hacene: Do you have any little problems, agitations, that maybe I can help you with?

Omar: Well...There is this man who keeps following me. He goes everywhere I go.

Hacene: Have you tried calling the police?

Omar: I called the police. I called the Fire Department, the Federal Bureau of Investigation, and the President of the United States.

Hacene: Did any of them help you?

Omar: The next day I didn't see the man anymore. I went outside to do my marketing. As soon as I turned the corner next to the A&P, I saw all these men.

Hacene: There are always men on the street.

Omar: No. They were watching me. They followed me all the way home. Ever since that day, five men have been watching me when I get undressed, at night when I lie alone in bed, they're even in my bathroom.

Hacene: Miss Fendermast, it's a common CUNT delusion that men are obsessed with CUNTS. It stems from the CUNT's knowledge that it is genitally inferior.

Omar: There are lots of men out here. *(Pointing to the audience and looking at them with wide eyes.)* They're all staring at me and they're waiting for me to take my clothes off.

Hacene *(knows he's got a real loony this time)*: Miss Fendermast, this is a private office. There's no one here but you and me.

Omar: There ARE men watching me. *(Calls out to the audience,)* Aren't all of you watching me?

   Lots of heckles from audience.

Hacene: Moreover, most men in this city aren't even interested in CUNTS. Now don't you think you're exaggerating? Just a little?

Omar: NO! *(Unconsciously sits down on the bed.)* I am not. Those men out there are watching me right now. I don't know why they are. I've never done anything to invite their glances and leers. I'm a good CUNT. I live alone. I never let anyone see me *(it stumbles over the word* naked) without my clothes on.

Hacene: Your mother?

Omar: Especially a MAN. For the last 32 years before I get undressed, I pull down the shades and I close all the curtains in the house. I lock the front door and the door to my bedroom. *(It's getting itself in a trance; its voice becomes slower evener.)* I sit on my bed and fold my hands. I start at the first button. I slowly unbutton my sweater. *(It starts slowly, unbuttoning its gray cashmere sweater. Its large provocative breasts, uplifted by a black lace half-bra, burst through the slowly opening sweater)*...I'm very tired because I've been typing so hard all day...I look up from unbuttoning my sweater for a second time and I see these MEN...(the palms of its hands rest on the black lace over its full nipples. When the palms of its hands move away, the nipples pop forward)...five big men's faces and their eyes are on my eyes...

Hacene *(staring rigidly at its gorgeous boobs)*: Are you sure their eyes are on your EYES, Miss Fendermast?

Omar: I don't want to see them, but I have to. They're THERE! I can see their nasty businessmen's cops' pupils travelling up down my misting flesh...(*its hands delicately lightly play with the tips of its nipples: brush the tips, flick a shudder, the almost nonexistent shudder in the world; a flick of the pointed tip of a red fingernail on that animal. Its hands press down its breasts and rub, smoothly, evened-outstrokes...*) I run into a corner. There's a man!

The psychiatrist is obviously as aroused as every man in the audience of the sex show. His right hand lightly strokes the double-knit material over his cock

Omar: This man isn't only STARING into my eyes. He's going to touch me! His hands are going to pin me against the wall. Huge blobs of water drop from these hands. The breath on my face is hot. He becomes larger as he walks one step...two step...(*it's now in a total trance*) his right hand insinuates itself between my sheer nylon panties and my open skin and tears...(*it tears at its underpants*)...he rips my panties into shreds... shreds of floating black cloth...

The psychiatrist's cock is standing bright red rigid outside his open fly. The psychiatrist's right hand is moving rapidly up and down the knob of this cock there are squishing sounds.

Omar: I have to do everything the man tells me. He tells me to stick the third finger of my right hand up my pussy. I stick the third finger of my right hand up my pussy. (*It sticks the third finger of its right hand up its pussy. At that point it goes crazy and can no longer use language. Its legs thrash wet. It's finger flies in and out touches its clit back down where it aches the clit aches; its mouth clamps down wet, safe, on the hard little nipple button its hand holds up, getting what it wants and at the same time wanting: the tip of its finger is now only touching the tip of its clit. Slowly now. Don't lose the concentration. Have to learn to relax totally so you become your finger. You become that hard little thing that is giving pleasure. That hard little thing is able to give perfect pleasure. That hard little thing is inducing an amazing orgasm and has to move much faster. If you let yourself feel this orgasm, you'll lose it. That hard little thing is IT. That hard little thing is IT.*) (*The world; the universe; perfection.*) Oh.

(*breathy*) Oooooh. Oh yes. Yes. Please...Yes. Yes. Oh my god. I want. (*The wave of sensation lowers.*) One more time. Oh. Oh. Oh yes I. (*The wave hits a peak lower than the first apex, drops into gray.*)

Hacene, (*before Omar recovers*): Suck me.

Omar: Santa Claus came to see me last night.

Hacene: Excuse me, Miss Fendermast?

Omar (*she knows this psychiatrist is a dope*): SANTA CLAUS visited me last night He visits me every night that I've been a good CUNT.

Hacene: How long has Santa Claus been visiting you?

Omar: Ever since I was a little CUNT. He likes me a lot. He tells me I'm not allowed to have anything to do with other men.

Hacene: Do you see Santa Claus often, Miss Fendermast?

Omar: I see him whenever he visits me. He comes down my chimney and says "Hi, Omar" and gives me my new present. Last week he came down head first. It was very confusing. I bandaged his head and gave him some camomile tea.

Hacene: What do you and Santa Claus talk about, Miss Fendermast?

Omar: We don't talk at all. We play "horsey" and "doctor". I like to play "prison" best. It's new.

Hacene: "Prison"?

Omar: I'm the bad prisoner and Santa Claus is the CIA jailer. It's very political. Santa Claus says that nowadays everything is politically determined.

Hacene: Miss Fendermast, I believe you're living in total delusion. I'm going to show you what REAL life is.

This part of the show is very rough

Omar: I don't know why you're saying that, doctor. But I'll do whatever you say because everyone I know says I'm sick.

Hacene: I want you to take off your clothes while you sing PROUD MARY.

Omar: I don't want to do that! Anything but that!

Hacene: I' m your doctor, Miss Fendermast. Do you trust me totally?

Omar (*looking up at him with total trust in its beautiful face*): Yes, doctor.

Hacene: Then do what I tell you to do!

> *Play Blondie's GONNA GET CHA but not so loud, the words can't be heard.*

> *Omar stands up walks to FRONT RIGHT of stage. Music for GONNA GET CHA starts playing. It lip-syncs words and, at first clumsily, then gets into it, dances and strips. It's naked. It walks over to Hacene Suddenly it remembers it's a CUNT who isn't into sex. It reverts.*
> *MUSIC OFF*

Hacene: Lie down on this bed on your back and spread your legs. Wide.

Omar: Why do I have to do that? Is that part of the treatment?

Hacene: It's a treatment and here's the treat. (*Unzips his pants and places his hand on what looks like a monstrous bulge.*) Do you have some rubbers on you?

Omar: Rubbers? What do you need rubbers for? It isn't raining.

Hacene (*walks over to bed and lies on top of it*): You're so dumb, the only thing that'll penetrate you is this. (*Gets between its legs and pretends to shove his cock up THE CUNT.*)

Omar: Oh doctor. Oh doctor. Are you sure this is part of the treatment? It feels so good...(*They're pretending to fuck medium hard and medium fast. Their asses are towards the audience so the audience can't see anything.*) THE CUNT my mother always told me it was painful to be sick.

Hacene: The pain'll come later, honey.

Omar: Oh. Oh.

Hacene: Ooooh. Oooh Miss Fendermast.

Omar: Please doctor. More in that place. Right there. Yes. Yes. A little over. Oh. Oh.

Hacene: Yees. Goddam you CUNT (*spreads into continual low rumbles.*)

Omar: Oh. Oh no. Oh Oh Oh (*higher in pitch*) Oh Oh Ah Ah Aaaah Aaah Oh yes (*lower*) Ooh? Ooh? Ooh. ooooh-oooh-ooh Ah. Aaaaghgh. (*It flops .*)

> *Hacene pulls up his black underpants, stands up and looks down on it*

Hacene: I'm going to give you exactly what you want, Miss Fendermast, cause I'm the best there is.

Omar: Wasn't that everything? (*in a total daze. With pure love in its voice. Its legs spread-eagled to the audience:*) I love you.

Hacene: I want you to come down here (*pointing to the stage floor in front of him*) and crouch down like a poodle.

Omar: Huh?

Hacene: Do you love me?

Omar: Yes.

Hacene: Then go down on all fours.

Omar: O. K . . (*There's a question in its voice. It gets down on all fours. It realizes it's a dog. It races back to its bed.*) No, I won't. I won't do that.

Hacene: Miss Fendermast, I'm still your doctor. Either you do exactly what I tell you to or you'll never see me again.

Omar, madly in love with him, looks at him. It goes back down on all fours.

Omar: Woof. Woof. (*As it lifts up its back leg to pee, Hacene is reaching for its ass and his thick cock is just about to touch the hole. Omar, freaking out again, runs behind the red velvet curtain,*) I want to go back to THE CUNT mommy in Hicksville! It never told me life would be like this.

The red velvet curtains close. Hacene in his psychiatrist suit and Omar in its uptown shopping outfit walk on stage in front of the red velvet curtains.

Hacene: Well. Miss Fendermast, do you still believe in Santa Claus?

Omar: Of course I do, doctor. If there wasn't a Santa Claus, I'd never get any presents.

⑦

A   C U N T   DOES NOT BELONG TO ANY MAN

I want to settle down. I want to tell all my boyfriends NO because fucking different men often emotionally confuses me: I stop differentiating between cock and cock. I don't know what I feel for any man except for whatever exact peculiar friendship exists for me at that moment between myself and the man. When vibrations move too fast and jagged- that kind of experience-, " I" move so fast, I can no longer feel. Is feeling therefore just self-reflection? I have to base myself on immediate strong action reactions, not on thoughts. I want to be calm cause then I have more freedom. I want one man I love deeply and proudly that is my focus.

I can swing on an idea as on a cord: my desire which is the idea during this time renders me the ideal obedient servant I will never escape this bond until success comes. Then there will be no idea, without responsibility duty appointments. My world: the world will be total ruin. My mind obeys only emotion, not emotion as opposed to intellect, but passion joy madness. Passion is the breaking up of rationality.

My passion lies in such things as sex, more and more sex: the force power I can perceive rises up outside me. I break myself against it. I am religious.

THE CUNT is pale. It's gained five pounds, all of its body movements are nervous. It is wearing a simple clinging blue-and-white print European sheath and a pair of high-heeled sandals. It is walking down the white steps to the Casbah entrance.

At the Rue de la Lyre entrance, ten French policemen are cornering an Algerian because he has no papers.

The Algerian cries out. The French policemen put their hands on him. The Algerian, frightened, struggles to escape. Now the Algerian crowd pushes against the police because they can't do anything else to say NO. The police are dragging the handcuffed Algerian with them.

THE CUNT immerses itself in the crowd. It's carring a black leather cosmetic case as if it's a bag of groceries. It realizes it doesn't know how to carry the case and this makes it more awkward.

THE CUNT'S the one up before the French border control. The French cops want to see its I.D. They're being rather nervous because of the recent incident with the Algerian. THE CUNT hands them I.D. One cop hands it back to it and signals it to pass. Then the cop stops it. He wants to examine its cosmetic case. THE CUNT makes itself flirt with the cop. It successfully draws his attention away from the cosmetic case and it gets through the border control.

It is walking down a wider empty street in the European section. It walks into a bar called the Milk Bar on the corner of Place Bugeaud. A lot of young hip Europeans are dancing and swinging around in this bar.The jukebox plays GONNA GET 'CHA by Blondie.

THE CUNT looks down at the jukebox songs. It puts the black leather cosmetic case on the floor so it can choose songs. Its foot pushes the cosmetic case under the jukebox. It pushes some buttons. It leaves the bar before the songs start.

Outside, on the Rue d'Isly, the Milk Bar jukebox can be heard playing GONNA GET 'CHA. Three European men walk into the bar. The bar explodes.

Because of the explosion, the useless crime by a single mad desperate my loneliness my madness my desperation my refusal to hide who I am from myself my refusal to hide TOTAL ANGER, the police begin to persecute the Algerians in the Casbah actively, the Europeans kill Algerians; we are forced together even though we hate each other because we are so lonely frightened unsure defensive because we have to survive.

141

IMMORAL

DECISION Nº. 3659
OF SEPTEMBER 18, 1986,
RELEASED IN THE FEDERAL REGISTER NO. 181
OF SEPTEMBER 30, 1986

The Federal Inspection Office for Publications Harmful to Minors
decided at its 333th meeting held on September 18, 1986, that:

Acker, Kathy,
Tough Girls Don't Cry, (*Blood and Guts in High School*)
Pocketbook No. 18/41 of the series
Heyne Scene
Wilhelm Heyne Publishing House, Munich

to be added to the list of publications harmful to minors.

Present at the meeting:

Chairman-Assistant Executive Officer Rudolf Stefen
Associate Member for the Arts - Professor Konrad Jentzsch
Associate Member for Literature - Academic Director
Horst Scheffler
Associate Member for Book Retail - Bookdealer
Wolfgang Hüster
Associate Member for Publishers - none
Associate Member for Youth Organisations - Sociologist
Wilfried Pohler
Associate Member for Youth Welfare - Clerk
Karl-Otto Lindlahr
Associate Member for the School Teachers - Principal
Günther Roland
Associate Member for the Churches - none
Associate Member for the State of Bavaria - Principal
Dr. Heinrich

Associate Member for the City of Berlin - Social Welfare Counsel
Dieter Punt
Associate Member for the City of Bremen - Social Welfare
Inspector Wolfgang Lindemeyer
Secretary - Clerk Marianne Romers
For the Petitioner - none
For the Defense - Dr. Wolfdieter Kuner. Esq.

THE CIRCUMSTANCES:

The main character is Janey, a precocious ten-year old girl. She lives with her father and is to him wife and daughter in one. Father and daughter frequently have sexual intercourse; at times Janey gives him a "blow job", sometimes "he fucks her in the ass" (p. 26) because she had a vaginal infection. Her father, however, falls in love with another woman. Finally he does not want her to be around any longer and sends her off to school in New York City to be sure she doesn't return to Mexico.

In New York she joins a gang, "The Scorpions." She gets in touch with drugs, alcohol, she has two abortions and likes masochistic acts. Together with the gang she commits offenses and crimes.

At the age of 13 she still lives in New York, in the slum quarters of the East Village. She still wants to "fuck around" as often as possible, she has sexual encounters with an 80-year-old writer. Anal intercourse takes place including masochistic acts. One day while masturbating, two burglars enter her apartment. They kidnap her and bring her to a Persian man.

The Persian wants to train her to become a whore. She is supposed to learn to fuck well, to do blow jobs and to be able to guess what her customers want from her without having to ask. For the entire period of time she lives in a dark room. One day she finds a pencil stub and an old note book and starts to write down her life story. She also finds a Persian grammar and begins to learn Persian. Pages 92ff. of her story are in Persian and German side by side. For the vast part it consists of individual words, mostly childish blabber that doesn't make any sense. A primitive vocabulary from her close environment is replicated. Beat up, eat, rob, kill, cunt, cock, etc. are penciled down.

Janey falls in love with the Persian. She keeps writing. On pages 130ff texts written by herself are printed, mostly incoherent fragments like: shit, I stink, puke, suck me. The texts and word fragments circle around the issues: relations to others, sex, disease.

The Persian slave trader considers her training finished but doesn't want to employ her as a perfect whore because in the meantime she got cancer.

Janey meets the writer Jean Genet. She travels with him, works in the fields of rich people, she is put into prison where she holds imaginary conversations with the guards. She turns blind and finally dies.

On the first 80 pages of the book mostly full page drawings depict male and female sex organs. Such drawings are found on pages 8, 16, 18, 24, 28, 30, 34, 38, 60, 62, 64, 80, 82, 201.

The structure of the plot is in part quite difficult to understand. It is partially very hard or completely impossible for the reader to see whether we are dealing with the protagonist's imagination or real events.

The author is using a number of "styles," except for the depiction of drawings: on page 26ff beginning with "A few hours later..." some paragraphs are printed six times, each with differing subsequent dialogues. On page 32 two sentences with identical wording are printed consecutively. On page 35 there is an insert by the author. Some thoughts and comments of the protagonist (or in italics) are highlighted. On pages 36 and 37 the author comments her own dialogues. In another text the main character describes herself as a "Lousy mindless salesgirl." On page 55 some sentences end with the word "SPLIT." On pages 86ff there is a constant change of scenes between Hester's novel and her own life story.

Some text are shown in the form of stanzas. In some poems you find sentences contrary to the grammatic rules. Often there are words in bold print, some texts are shown only in capital letters. The protagonist imagines being another person, for instance the writer Erica Jong on page 159. On page 163 the plot is structured like stage scenes. The final chapter consists almost completely of drawings with few written additions. They do not make sense by itself.

The novel of the author has generated varied responses. For instance she has been accused of having copied parts of Pauline Réages' book "The Story of O." (the novel "The Story of O." was put on the list of publications hamrful to minors by decision No. 1942 of November 3, 1967).

In the magazine "Wolkenkratzer [Skyscraper] Art Journal" of January 11, 1986, Karin Haderhold points out that "language is first of all a method of verbal communication, at any given time in daily life, but it can also be alienated and lifted to a level where it works as communication in the sense of emotional contact. This kind of literature utilizes texts and functions like a distorting mirror." The [newspaper] Aachener Illustrierte, issue 2/86, remarks: "It is a pity that if a woman throws herself into literary chasms she cannot come up with any varieties or excesses going beyond traditional male fantasies."

REASONS

The petition for putting the book on the Index is justified. The book in question, "Tough Girls Don't Cry" is to be added to the list of publications harmful to minors.

The pocketbook is harmful to minors according to paragraph 1, 1 of the Law for the Protection of Minors (GjS). It is confusing in terms of sexual ethics and is therefore equal to "immoral texts" according to paragraph 1, 1 GjS.

In this novel the young protagonist, Janey, gets in touch with sexual intercourse early in her life. Already at the age of 10 she has sexual intercourse with her father. As was shown in detail, they are also having anal intercourse, cunnilingus and fellatio. Child sex as well as incest are belittled by these descriptions. During her subsequent, quite brief life, sexual intercourse is the primary consideration. Already before she has been trained to be a perfect whore, who can read the desires of men before they are expressed, she loves first of all sado-masochistic acts.

Also in many other instances the author expresses her pleasure in sado-masochistic acts. On pages 162ff it says:

> I don't call having some young boy between my sheets SEX. I rarely let myself go for young or nice boys because I know I'll get bored. I want the textures of your lives, the complexities set up by betrayals and danger- I like men who hurt me because I don't always see myself, I have my egotism cut up. I love this: I love to be beaten up and hurt and taken on a joy ride. This SEX— what I call SEX—guides my life. I know this Sex of traitors, deviants, scum, and schizophrenics exists. They're the ones I want.

Passages like these are not only youth threatening but also dangerous for adults. According to paragraph 18, 3 of the Criminal Code (StGB) the distribution of sado-masochistic literature is to be punished and by this the legislature made clear that media containing such materials go far beyond the limits of what is harmful to minors.

Her stories and Persian poems written in Cyrillic script deal with sexual themes, too. The following may demonstrate this:

يك صُندُل بِرو، يك أطاق
و، يك پَنجَرۀ و، يك پَنجَرۀ
و، يك پَنجَرۀ و، يك پَنجَرۀ
بيستر نيست

The only thing is a cunt and a cock.

The pocketbook does not only multiply sexual intercourse with children and incest which is punishable according to paragraph 173 of the Criminal Code, it does not only glorify fellatio, cunnilingus and anal intercourse, but it also renders a positive picture of deviant pathological sexual acts. Sexual excitement is increased by sado-masochistic acts. This is, among other things, the basic message of the novel. This kind of description gives reason to worry that the still unformed juvenile readers will be hampered from becoming fully responsible personalities and sexual partners, i.e. readers who are not yet strengthened by experience and have not yet reached sufficient intellectual maturity in their values as well as in their analytical faculties and more so who are subject to distinct tensions and sensibilities especially in the realm of eroticism and sexuality.

The threat to young people that derives in this book from the written rendition of deviant and perverse sexual acts is multiplied by the drawings. The obvious depictions do not leave anything to the reader's imagination.

The threat to young people through the depiction of pornographic acts and such drawings is aggravated by the description and belittlement of abortions. The protagonist Janey has altogether two abortions. The abortion by a quack is described on pages 41ff.

No exceptions can be granted in accordance with paragraph 1, 2 GjS. The pocketbook "Tough Girls Don't Cry" is neither art nor does it serve any artistic purpose, since a text can only be considered art if it maintains a certain level of artistic standards. This decision is not only based purely on aesthetic criteria but also according to the importance which a work of art has for the pluralistic society and its ideas about the function of art in society. These limitations of the freedom of artistic expression are justified by the constitutional principle to honor human dignity. "Part of this is to protect juveniles from moral dangers. Particularly contemporary art is in many ways not easy to comprehend (BGH GA 1961, 240) since it contains elements of provocation and aggression. The effects that are triggered through the confrontation with this kind of art works for the intellectual and spiritual development of a not yet fully matured person are not only arduous and depressive but also dangerous according to paragraph 1, 1 GjS. The law can assume that the mature citizen is able to make responsible decisions whether to encounter this type of art work. Children and juveniles are not able to make responsible decisions of this sort. If the legal community therefore makes this decision for them then society fullfills the youth's right to be protected from an inappropriate confrontation with art." (BVerwGE [Federal Administrative Court Decision] 39, 196)

The above described standards are missing in this book. The author is using a number of styles to write her novel. She uses poems, Persian script, etc., as stylistic elements. The banal street language is used. The author describes the life of Janey in the book, her gradual demise could be interpreted as a consequence of missing personal relationships if it weren't for her death by cancer. The book argues against capitalist society, it claims that rich people have all the power, with money - and only with money - the world can be changed. It attacks the commercial exploitation of sexuality. The discrimination of women is condemned in brief sequences. Janey says men teach women ways they want them to be. Janey, however, is the only female person who appears in the book; she has an exclusive male fixation, she has nothing in mind but men, except for her intention to go to high school.

The chosen elements of style do not enhance the novel to the level of art. A colorful, exciting and yet banal and trivial gutter language in itself cannot relay any artistic qualities within a novel.

The novel merely mirrors social problems without being genuinely creative in any way. It is also remarkable that Kathy Acker who considers herself a "feminist" - as she is frequently championed - examines less the role of women her novel than mostly deals with male power and potency. The [newspaper] Aachener Illustrierte in issue No. 2/86 charged her with having no new idea exceeding or varying traditional male phantasies. The newspaper says that "she was hatching some crap" which, literally, was only remarkable due to the reading-presentation by the author.

After being confronted with the fact that she had already written pornography before and performed in sex shows she was accused of imitating traditional literature. She was quoted by her own lines: "Blood and guts [from the original title] was an attempt to experiment with writing."

All this makes clear that this novel does not reach the level worthy to be of value to the pluralistic society. The protection of young people takes precedence over the dissemination of this work as art.

Translation by Frank Mecklenburg

SEMIOTEXT(E) · NATIVE AGENTS SERIES
Chris Kraus, *Editor*

69 Ways to Play the Blues Jürg Laederach

Soft Subversions Félix Guattari

Speed and Politics Paul Virilio

Still Black, Still Strong Dhoruba Bin Wahad, Mumia Abu-Jamal & Assata Shakur

Why Different?: A Culture of Two Subjects Luce Irigaray

SEMIOTEXT(E) • ACTIVE AGENTS SERIES
Chris Kraus & Sylvère Lotringer, *Editors*

The Empire of Disorder Alain Joxe

Printed in the United States
by Baker & Taylor Publisher Services